Greg had ev[...]
kissing Jacl[...]

He'd been dying to taste [...] she'd strutted through the restaurant.

Just when he'd been sizing up the situation, taking in her every curve and nuance so he could wring out every possible bit of pleasure from it for both of them, Jackie plastered herself against him for the most mind-blowing kiss he'd ever experienced.

She was like a sensory explosion, swamping every inch of him with tantalizing sensations. Her lips swayed over his in slow undulations, leaving him no choice but to seek entrance to her mouth for a more thorough taste.

Sweet and complex. Jackie tasted like a dessert wine and left him hungering for more.

But all the while he tried to drink in her taste, she was tormenting his chest with the soft nudge of her breasts. He could envision those breasts, those upturned nipples, perfectly.

And the image was killing him.

"Jackie?" He pulled away in slow degrees. They were in the middle of the sidewalk, for crying out loud. He kissed her one last time before backing up a step. He wanted to go upstairs with her and unveil her body at his leisure, not maul her in full view of her neighbors.

She smiled before she opened her eyes. "Hmm?"

"Do you mind if I come inside?"

Dear Reader,

A bachelor party seems an unlikely place to find romance, until the best man runs off with the reluctant stripper....

Ever had a mortifying moment that makes you wish you could rewind for just a few minutes? Jackie Brady, heroine of *Revealed*, runs into a doozy! I hope you enjoy her bachelor party mishap and the classy way she maneuvers herself out of the situation.

Because this gutsy, unconventional woman appealed to me on so many levels, I had to make it up to her somehow. Please let me know if you think I was sufficiently kind in sending sexy Greg De Costa her way! Greg is as committed to the fast track as Jackie is determined to forge her own path, however, so don't expect their road to romance to be smooth.

While you are reading, I'll be busy putting the finishing touches on my upcoming May 2003 Blaze title, *Wild and Wicked,* the sequel to *Wild and Willing,* Blaze #54. Visit me at www.JoanneRock.com to learn more about my future releases or to let me know what you think of this book. I'd love to hear from you!

Happy reading!

Joanne Rock

Books by Joanne Rock

HARLEQUIN TEMPTATION
863—LEARNING CURVES
897—TALL, DARK AND DARING

HARLEQUIN BLAZE
26—SILK, LACE &
    VIDEOTAPE
48—IN HOT PURSUIT
54—WILD AND WILLING

REVEALED
Joanne Rock

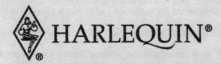

TORONTO • NEW YORK • LONDON
AMSTERDAM • PARIS • SYDNEY • HAMBURG
STOCKHOLM • ATHENS • TOKYO • MILAN • MADRID
PRAGUE • WARSAW • BUDAPEST • AUCKLAND

To my brother Neil, who reads Kant and Nietzsche, and now me! Thank you for caring about my work.

And to Dean, for providing endlessly entertaining insights into the male perspective.

ISBN 0-373-69119-X

REVEALED

Copyright © 2003 by Joanne Rock.

1

JACKIE BRADY STARTED TO panic when her tail fell off for the third time. Thank God for duct tape or her fuzzy pants could have well been down around her ankles before she danced her way into the restaurant.

She finished her costume adjustments and smoothed her glued-on whiskers just as the elevator doors slid open. Careful not to tread on her ailing tail, she stepped into the penthouse-level eatery of a downtown Boston brownstone. Now all she needed to do was locate the birthday boy, sing her telegram song, and then she could reclaim her Friday night as her own.

So what if her stint as a singing telegram wasn't exactly rocket science? It paid more than her daytime work as a copywriter. Both jobs were only a means to an end anyway. She was prepared to abide a few sacrifices to achieve her dream of composing children's music.

Besides, there was a certain nobility in any job that involved making people happy. A nobility that could scarcely be diminished by the kitty ears perched on her head.

The squeak of her tennis shoes on the polished wooden floor resounded throughout the dining area. Patrons paused between bites of mozzarella sticks and greasy chicken wings to note the cat woman strolling in their midst.

Not that Jackie cared.

But then, she'd been causing too much commotion all of her life. There was the time she decided to sing the elements of the periodic table for her science fair project. Sure she'd ruffled the feathers of all the kids who'd made robots, but she'd taken second place at the state competition. Then, just last week she'd gone out on a limb at a singing audition by transforming a rendition of a melodic herbal store jingle into a semi-tuneful Tarzan-inspired jungle cry.

Jackie was no stranger to turning heads. Or taking risks. Sometimes they paid off, like the science fair victory. Sometimes they landed her back on the pavement singing telegrams, as last week's unsuccessful audition proved.

Still, she wondered how she'd gotten suckered into this last-minute singing assignment when all she'd wanted to do tonight was recharge her creative batteries and develop some new song concepts. She'd had an idea rattling around in her brain—some rough lyrics for a new diet soda commercial she would polish and put on her demo tape. But the Zing-O-Gram office temp had sounded so desperate when she'd called, Jackie had no choice but to cover tonight's late-breaking gig.

Just her luck, she had to be the only Zing-O-Gram employee on call without a date lined up for a Friday night. Nothing new there. Sure she had plenty of offers. Heck, the cat getup on its own could usually elicit a few dinner invitations in the course of an evening.

But never from the right sort of guys. Jackie wanted a man who knew how to have a good time—someone who cared more about following his heart and his dreams than the Almighty Buck. Boston was full of gorgeous men, but they all seemed to be on a relentless career fast-track that Jackie refused to enter.

Too bad.

So she would locate Gregory the birthday boy, sing him a cute song for his special day, and be on her way back to her solo Friday night. She'd be fine without a man in her life, and she'd be fine getting through tonight's performance.

Assuming she didn't burst a seam on this two-sizes-too-small cat costume first.

Jackie took slow, shallow breaths to ensure the black fuzzy suit stayed in place. She could handle this as long as she kept her song in a manageable octave. Those high notes had been known to strain even the best of seams—she sure as heck wasn't about to try shattering any glass outfitted in this feline shrink-wrap. She'd just keep the tune in a comfortable range and she'd have no problem staying in her garb.

She was singing a simple ditty at a birthday party for a six-year-old boy. What could possibly go wrong?

"MAYBE SHE GOT THE address wrong," Greg De Costa shouted into the cell phone. He couldn't hear a damn thing over the music set at full blast in a back room of Flanagan's.

Struggling to keep the phone against his ear while he wrestled open a new bottle of champagne, Greg ducked out of the way of a rogue dart sent sailing through the bar by a soused partygoer. He didn't mean to hassle the office worker at Zing-O-Gram, but the stripper he'd ordered for his brother's bachelor party was almost half an hour late.

Where was she?

The masses were starting to get restless. If he didn't produce a naked woman soon, he'd definitely lose his audience. As the general manager for one of Boston's major television stations, Greg couldn't abide any event—televised or otherwise—that didn't hold its own in the ratings. He would dance on the tables himself before he lost his viewers.

Although, no doubt, a naked woman would probably capture a larger share of the bachelor party market.

After grilling the harried woman at Zing-O-Gram for a few more minutes, Greg folded up the phone and popped another cork just as his brother stepped out of the crowd.

Mike De Costa—future bridegroom—claimed an open bottle of top-shelf champagne and proceeded to drink it as if it were a longneck. He grimaced at the label. "Since when do bachelors chug drinks with bubbles?"

"Since they have something big to celebrate, like marriage to a woman who's nice enough to put up with you." Greg had known Mike's bride since kindergarten. Hannah Williams was as sweet as they came—

and far too good for a guy determined to charm his way through life like Mike.

Mike swung his arms, sloshing champagne in a wide arc around himself as he did. "But look at what a catch she's getting," he protested.

"All six feet, two inches of burning ambition and refined taste," Greg acknowledged, rolling his eyes.

Mike called up a belch from his toes and grinned. "You probably got me on the refined taste thing," he admitted. "But not every woman cares about burning ambition, you know."

"No?" Greg popped the cork on the last champagne bottle and handed it over to the waiter filling a tray of glasses.

"No." Mike exchanged his half-finished liter bottle for a beer. "But obviously women like that are a foreign species to you."

"I never met a species of woman I didn't like." Greg mopped off the bar with the waiter's towel, a habit engrained long ago, in another bar, in another life. "I'm just not about to get serious with anyone who doesn't understand how important it is to get ahead."

"Then you're a confirmed bachelor until you find an MBA-carrying superwoman. You've been trying to get ahead ever since the first moment you cut in front of me in line at the candy store."

"Not this time," Greg corrected him, reaching for Mike's vacated bottle of champagne. "You're ahead of me in the matrimony department with a wedding coming up in three weeks. You're more than welcome to stay in first place."

Truer words were never spoken. Greg needed a serious relationship like he needed his old bartending job back.

Not in this lifetime. Greg's job was the envy of all his friends. He'd worked his butt off to carve a niche for himself among Boston's business elite, and entanglements with the female persuasion only seemed to complicate things. What woman wanted to stick around while he worked until midnight in the studio to get just the right sound for a new commercial or wined and dined clients every weekend? After too many failed relationships and pissed-off women, Greg had learned to keep relationships simple and...brief.

His gig as a network general manager was a coup he planned to enjoy to the fullest—something he didn't have any intention of risking for the sake of a woman.

The bachelor life couldn't be any sweeter. To toast that fact, Greg gladly tipped the bottle to his lips, savoring the perfect finish of good champagne.

A ruckus on the other side of the bar caught his attention. Flanagan's had a dining room at one end, a big bar in the middle, and a back room with a pool table for private parties. From his vantage point near the dartboard, Greg spied a small sea of turning heads, heard the slow rise of collective wolf whistles over the blaring music.

Greg couldn't see the sudden center of attention with the throng of men to block his view, but he guessed either the stripper had arrived, or someone had smuggled a sexy power tool into the bar for his friends to admire.

Chances were, Zing-O-Gram had finally come through for him.

Downing another short swig from the champagne bottle—his last sip for the night so he could keep a clear head to stay in control of the party—Greg said a mental thank-you to the new arrival. Now that the stripper was here, he could move the evening along and hopefully salvage a few hours afterward to go over some demo tapes at home. As much as he wanted to ensure his brother had a good time, Greg hadn't risen to the top of the heap at the television station by putting in the standard forty-hour work weeks. He had to review a three-mile-high stack of audio demos in a search for some fresh voice-over talent.

No sooner had he formed the thought than his senses were bombarded by the sexiest voice he'd ever heard.

"But I'm looking for Gregory..." a sultry feminine alto protested. "Is Gregory here?"

Howls of laughter emanated from the horde of males.

"Sure he's here, honey." Mike stepped into the fray. "He's going to be real happy to see you."

"I *am* supposed to deliver a Zing-O-Gram here, right?" Her gorgeous voice sailed over Greg's senses. She had the sexy rasp of a torch singer.

Mike smiled, attempting to straighten his lopsided tie as he flashed her a killer grin. "We've been waiting for you."

Greg slid off the bar stool, still squinting into the crowd to get a glimpse of the woman behind that incredible voice. After having cut his professional teeth in radio, Greg could recognize a memorable set of pipes. The anonymous stripper had them.

The sea of men approached Greg and Flanagan's back room wearing interchangeable goofy grins. Greg had the feeling from their expressions that he was going to get his money's worth for tonight's performance. The stripper must be pretty hot to inspire such fawning before she'd wriggled out of her dress.

Mike reached Greg first. He clapped his brother on the shoulder and winked, then reached into the crowd. "Here's Gregory, honey. He's the man responsible for the party. I think he's ready for the show."

Mike pulled a female from the crowd. Men parted to make room for her and her...tail?

Greg took a quick inventory of the performer he'd ordered to please tonight's bachelor party crowd. Weathered black kitty ears nestled into the woman's silky, cinnamon-colored hair. Bright green eyes peered back at him over long black whiskers that were slightly askew. A pink triangle artfully painted over the woman's nose completed the feline aspect.

She might have looked like she'd danced straight off the *Barney* set if she hadn't been wearing an R-rated cat costume that hugged every curvy nuance of her body.

Greg swallowed as he took in the exposed tops of her breasts, thrust up high by an outfit that had to be too small for this generously endowed creature. The only place she seemed to have any breathing room was around her waist, a tiny curve that nipped in substantially from her rounded hips.

Who knew how long his eyes lingered over those hips. Why was it the furry black getup looked sexier than any showy combination of lace and satin?

Maybe it was the tail that wound around one hip and settled along her thigh, all the way down to her...tennis shoes. Hell, he saw Nike stock in his future. The long rope of black fur seemed to stroke and caress her leg with every breath the woman took.

Meow.

Perhaps he'd taken too long admiring her...outfit. Before he could introduce himself, the cat woman stuck out her hand.

"Hi." She squeezed his fingers in a cool, professional grip. "I'm Jackie, the entertainment. This is your party?"

Her voice slithered over him, reminding him of smoky blues cafés and sultry jazz singers.

He nodded. He'd hired her after all. "I'm Greg." Technically, it was Mike's party. But her bill no doubt had Greg's name on it. Besides, he wasn't quite ready to turn her over to Mike's friends just yet.

There was something compelling about Jackie the cat woman-stripper. Some classy, complex edge that her whiskers and kitty ears couldn't diminish.

She frowned for a moment. "I see. Zing-O-Gram has been a bit overloaded this week. Sorry about the confusion."

"Not a problem," Greg assured her, honestly. Her late arrival hadn't thrown off his schedule too much. "You're here now and that's all that matters. Can I get you a drink or anything else before you get started?"

Why did he find himself wanting to delay her show? Sure he was wildly curious about the body she was hiding underneath that kitten costume. But the notion of her being so completely revealed in a bar with all of Mike's horny friends looking on suddenly disturbed him.

He'd heard of college students earning money for their tuition this way. Is that what had convinced Jackie to don the cat suit?

Jackie licked her lips, a gesture that seemed to suit her feline garb.

Greg tracked the progress of that small, pink tongue and found his own mouth had gone dry as dust.

"I wouldn't mind a glass of water." She glanced longingly at the bar.

Twenty guys shouted to the bartender for water.

Jackie shuffled on her tennis shoes as if nervous. Her tail seemed to twitch in response, drawing his attention unerringly to her long legs.

If Greg didn't know better, he'd swear he was drunk. Since when did a stripper in a two-bit cat costume turn him on to this extreme? He was twisted in knots before she'd shed so much as a glove.

He rolled his shoulders in an attempt to work out one of those knots. Maybe he'd just been working too hard lately. He hadn't been out on a date since his disastrous break up with the lady meteorologist...three months ago?

Obviously he was sex-starved. He just hadn't realized it until Jackie had strutted her way into his life.

But he had no intention of acting on an impulsive attraction to a seductive pussycat.

Poor choice of images.

He tried in vain to staunch the blatantly sexual thoughts bombarding his senses. He needed to give Jackie her water and then allow her free rein to do her show.

Surely once she launched into her practiced routine of seduction, Greg would lose interest. Then he could get his mind off her...tail, and back on business.

JACKIE TUCKED HER TAIL closer to her body and gulped down her water gratefully.

The cat costume had never felt blatantly erotic until Greg De Costa had looked at her in it.

The man had her overheating, inside and out, and the soaring temperature didn't have anything to do with being embarrassed at her birthday party snafu.

No. Jackie didn't care that a bunch of overgrown boys had hired her to sing at their friend's birthday party. She was used to being the center of attention and their ogling stares didn't ruffle her fur in the least.

But Greg De Costa was another story.

One look at the man had her hyperventilating—not a good thing in a costume held together with duct tape.

He was handsome in a Tom Cruise sort of way—he had the look of a cocky Boston business exec, all charm and smooth talk and control. He wore a crisp white shirt tucked into navy-blue trousers with burgundy-striped suspenders. A matching wine-colored tie hung around his neck, but he'd loosened the knot at his throat and unbuttoned the collar.

Jackie had to admire the way his suntanned skin and dark-brown hair contrasted with that pristine white shirt. He probably summered on Martha's Vineyard and wintered at Vale. She knew the type well. Heck, she'd grown up surrounded by overprivileged men and couldn't find all that much to recommend them.

But those guys hadn't possessed Greg De Costa's penetrating brown eyes.

The charismatic birthday boy didn't look at her with the standard I-know-what-you-look-like-underneath-that-cat-costume stare. His frank gaze was at once more respectful and more intimate. He peered at her like he knew she'd rather be at home writing stanzas.

And like he'd rather be there with her.

The notion unsettled her far more than any obvious, meaningless ogling from the other twenty-some guys in Flanagan's.

She needed to shake Greg's mesmerizing stare, sing her song, and flee the bar before she did something stupid like wrap herself around him and start purring.

"I'm ready," she announced, taking the situation in hand. She'd already spent too long soaking up the heated vibes of attraction zipping between her and Greg. "Shall I set up over here?" She walked to a small dance floor in the corner of Flanagan's back room.

She could perform most anywhere, but she'd learned to take charge of her environment in this business. She liked a wall behind her, her audience in front of her. Besides, she felt more in control when she named her parameters.

The throng of men attending the party moved as one into the back room, dutifully situating themselves right where she wanted them.

She could do this. They really were as well behaved as the six-year-olds she usually performed for, even if they had greeted her with wolf whistles. At least they hadn't tried pulling her tail.

Greg was the last man to fall in line. He prowled the perimeter of the crowd, his eyes never leaving her.

"Do you need us to set up some music?" he called over the heads of his friends as they seated themselves at cocktail tables all around her.

"I'm the music," she announced, allowing her artistic pride to get the best of her for a moment.

She was no lip-synching performer, after all. Jackie wasn't here to dance around in a cat costume. She was here to sing.

No room full of overgrown boys was going to make her forget it. Though heaven knew, Greg De Costa was doing a damnably good job of trying.

She closed her eyes for a moment, willing away the sensual magnetism of Greg's eyes. She took a deep breath and quickly regretted it as the duct tape along her seam shifted under the pressure of expanding lungs.

Panic welled up in her at the thought of flashing a room full of men. She hadn't even been able to stuff a bra underneath her too-tight costume. If the duct tape gave, her audience would be in for an eyeful.

Jackie hummed out a middle "C," allowing the pure musical note to center her.

Three minutes and she'd be out of here. She could make it another three minutes without bursting out of her costume.

The musical note grew, reverberating through her. She relaxed and breathed, nearly forgetting about the duct tape, but not quite forgetting about Greg De Costa.

"Happy birthday to you..." Jackie launched into her song, a slightly revamped version of the birthday classic.

Was it her imagination, or did the room still once her voice hit the airwaves? Her audience grew less leering, more attentive as she belted out her song in perfect pitch.

Nothing like a good performance to soothe her nerves.

She vocalized her way into the last refrain, more confident with every note that she was going to make it out of Flanagan's back room with kitty costume and her dignity intact.

Then her eyes collided with Greg's.

His warm-coffee gaze wasn't offering up heated glances anymore. Unless you could call his intense, enraptured stare heated.

He liked her voice.

She knew it as surely as if he'd spoken the words aloud. Her vocal chords were her one and only vanity, the lone genetic gift from her prodigy parents.

Men—being such visual creatures—rarely recognized her single outstanding quality. But Greg De Costa knew it, heard it, admired it.

Her heart started pounding in a way that threatened her furry shrink-wrap. Blood pulsed through her, flushing every last inch of her body with liquid heat.

Oh no.

Desire swamped her along with the closing notes of her birthday song.

"Happy birthday, dear Gregory..." Dear God, had she just called him Gregory again? She'd meant to sing it as Greg.

Nervous embarrassment joined the swirl of musical notes and sensual hunger building in her veins.

"Happy birthday to..." Her chest hammered against fuzzy black fur as her song reached its final crescendo. The duct tape strained and stretched to hold the material of her costume together.

If she had any sense she would have risked singing off-key to save her outfit.

Damn her musical pride.

"...you!" Arms flung wide, she belted out the last note like a certified opera diva.

And froze in horror as her kitty costume slid all the way to her knees.

2

GREG HAD BLOWN OUT LOTS of candles in his day, but he'd never had a birthday wish come true so fast as tonight.

Sure, he'd wanted to see Jackie naked, but he'd been so hypnotized by her phenomenal voice, it took him a minute to realize she'd ditched her whole outfit in a bolder move than he'd ever seen any stripper attempt. No one else sang their way out of their outfit, of that much he was certain.

She'd stunned the crowd so much the guys around him forgot to whistle for one long moment. Hell, Greg forgot there was even anyone else in the room as he took in her completely bared breasts. Taut pink nipples tipped slightly upward, free from any bra or those little tasseled cups some strippers wore.

The only garment she sported underneath the fallen cat clothes were flame-red panties so small they could have served double duty as a postage stamp.

Despite the panties, she couldn't have looked any less like a stripper. She had curves in all the right places, but they probably weren't as generous as most women in her profession. Every inch of her creamy skin was perfect, without a beauty mark or false eyelash anywhere to detract from it.

But most unstripper-like of all—she appeared absolutely mortified to be on display in front of thirty salivating men.

One lone wolf whistle pierced through the crowd and shattered the silence along with Greg's greedy catalog of her every feature.

The sound seemed to jar the mostly naked cat woman as much as it startled Greg. Jackie folded her arms over herself to shield her body from her audience, giving Greg all the proof he needed that she didn't want to go through with her striptease.

Screw the audience approval ratings.

Ignoring the rapidly multiplying catcalls and whistles, Greg yanked a fresh tablecloth off of a nearby busboy's cart, disrupting at least ten glasses of champagne. With the flick of his wrist, he unfurled the white linen and cloaked Jackie's body in a crisp blanket.

A chorus of boos echoed through the crowd of Mike's half-baked friends.

Jackie turned grateful eyes toward Greg, cinching the makeshift cape around herself with slightly fumbling hands.

Some moron shouted from the back of the private room. "Take it off!"

An even bolder moron pushed his way to the front of the group, crunching broken glass under his feet from the disrupted bus boy's cart. "What the hell kind of striptease was that?"

"Show's over." Greg kept his body between Jackie and the inebriated masses, wishing like hell he had the option of just cutting to a commercial.

He reached for Jackie, figuring the best thing to do would be to whisk her out the back entrance.

"That was *not* a striptease," Jackie announced, standing on her toes to look over Greg's shoulder at her accuser. She was obviously recovering from her bout of stage fright. "*That* was an accident."

The vehemence in her voice seemed to catch the guy off guard as much as Greg.

"I'll say it was an accident." The guy turned his bleary-eyed attention toward Greg, lucky for his sorry butt. "You're trying to tell me that's all we get from the stripper?"

"I am *not* a stripper." Tennis shoes squeaked in a flurry of restless movement as Jackie fairly bristled right out of her tablecloth.

An unwelcome sense of relief washed over Greg. Why should he care whether she was or wasn't a stripper?

"Who are you?" Greg prompted, wondering what woman in her right mind would walk into a bachelor party clad as a cat.

She drew her compact self up to her full height. Her kitty ears just reached his nose but she packed a powerful glare with intense green eyes.

"I am the Zing-O-Gram." She enunciated every word with slow precision.

Greg bit his tongue to staunch the automatic laughter rising in his throat. He doubted anyone could make a Zing-O-Gram sound like a force to be reckoned with, but Jackie was doing a damn good job.

Even the drunken guy looked cowed before he

stalked off toward the pool table, muttering under his breath until they couldn't hear him anymore.

The rest of the crowd had failed to disperse however, and Greg didn't like the rumblings of discontent. He needed to get Jackie out of here, fast.

"Are you okay?"

"I think so." She hitched at the tablecloth around her shoulders, the black leggings of her costume still visible from her knee down. Apparently she had knotted the rest of the fallen outfit around her waist somehow. "Thanks to you."

Could he help it that her words made him stand taller? "You're really not a stripper?"

"I think I'm a few alphabets short of the right cup size to be an exotic dancer."

His natural inclination was to allow his gaze to wander over the breasts that had received more than a passing grade from him, but that didn't seem in keeping with his attempt to rescue her from a room full of horny bachelors. Greg closed his eyes instead, willing away memories of Jackie's perfect body.

He was surprised when he sensed her lean closer. Soft strands of her hair slid across his shoulder. A clean, sexy perfume teased his nose.

"That means no," she whispered in his ear. "I'm not a stripper."

A very happy circumstance, in Greg's book. Not that he hadn't dated a stripper—make that exotic dancer—or two in his day. He just had a difficult time reconciling Jackie to that kind of lifestyle.

Besides, he rather liked knowing she hadn't shared that perfect body with innumerable bachelor parties.

Greg peered around Flanagan's until he found an exit door in the back. He nodded toward the potential escape route.

"I vote we blow this joint. Do you mind if I walk you to your car to make sure you get there safely?"

"I'm with you." She squeezed the tablecloth to her body with determined fingers and squeaked her way across the polished wooden floor in her tennis shoes, head held high.

Greg followed in her wake glaring back at Mike's disgruntled friends as they grumbled over losing their entertainment.

Jackie's exit proved to be as memorable as her entrance. The cat woman might not be a stripper, but her sense of showmanship could give a seasoned stage veteran a run for the money as she sailed out the door, linen cape flying.

Greg noticed her ramrod straight posture deflated a bit once they'd made it through the exit and into a cramped stairwell, however. The slump lasted all of five seconds before Jackie turned on him and flashed him a sunny grin.

"I can handle it from here, Greg." She offered her hand as if to seal a bargain. "Thanks for helping me out of an awkward situation."

The strength of her citrusy perfume kicked up a notch in the small, dim space. Or maybe Greg was only more aware of her.

"I'd like to walk you to your car, if you don't mind."

He wasn't just saying it because he was attracted to her and her mile-long legs. No woman should navigate the streets of Boston in a shredded cat costume and a table-cloth.

"That's okay. If you could just point me in the direction of the ladies' room I'll try to make some repairs to my outfit." Her whiskers twitched as she spoke.

Greg fought the urge to smooth his fingers over them, to trace them from their tips to their source at the top of her full upper lip.

"I don't think your costume is in any shape to be repaired."

"Well, I can't exactly ride the metro in a tablecloth." Her crooked grin set the whiskers at a jaunty angle. "Besides, I need to retreat somewhere to check in with the Zing-O-Gram desk. I have the feeling our new office temp sent a stripper out to a six-year-old's birthday party and I'd like to make sure she doesn't unveil as much as I did tonight."

He had trouble focusing on her words. He was in a darkened stairwell with a half-naked woman and her perfume was driving him out of his mind. Greg found himself leaning closer, trying to catch a stronger whiff of her fragrance.

Too bad she was already retreating down the stairs.

"Bye." She managed a little wave, releasing the tablecloth with one hand for all of a nanosecond. "Thank you so much for coming to my rescue."

Confusion jolted him out of his mission to track her scent. She was leaving?

"Wait." He didn't know what he was going to say next, or how he was going to make her stay.

But Greg De Costa knew one thing for certain.

No matter that Jackie the Cat looked like walking mayhem, he wasn't ready to let her saunter out of his life just yet.

JACKIE PAUSED AND TURNED back, knowing she'd be hard pressed to deny the Adonis in corporate clothes just about anything. Had a tie ever looked so good slung around a man's neck? Jackie's eyes kept returning to the enticing hollow at the base of his throat, the hint of skin unveiled by one neglected top button.

He looked way too out of her league—the kind of man who dated women in understated Calvin Klein couture, not misfits in polyester kitty fur. Guys like Greg appreciated women who worked for Fortune 500 companies, women whose golf game was as low as their IQ was high.

Jackie, on the other hand, prided herself on always choosing the road less traveled or the man least likely to conform.

And Greg wasn't exactly a rabble-rouser. She barely knew him, but his designer tie and suspenders told a story of their own.

"Yes?" She could at least see what he wanted, however. Sure, he was all wrong for her. But he had saved her from extreme mortification in the bar.

Maybe he wanted to know her whole name.

Or her number.

Or maybe a night in her bed as compensation for his

gallant tablecloth rescue—a thought that didn't deter her as much as it should have.

He loomed over her, taller than her to start with, and now he stood two steps above her in the narrow stairwell. His eyes were so dark she could no longer discern their color, but they glistened back at her in the dim light.

"Let me at least drive you home."

"I'll be okay." The offer tempted her, but how could she accept a ride from a man she barely knew? A man who might have only been nice to her because he thought she'd be grateful. "But thank you."

"Do you know someone who can come pick you up?" Greg's brow furrowed as he frowned, the gesture adding all sorts of interesting lines to his face.

Jackie shook her head before realizing she should probably just say anything to extricate herself from this awkward social situation politely. The man was proving difficult to shake, but some part of her responded to his concern for her, too.

Jackie had always been good at drawing attention to herself—whether she'd intended to or not. But she'd never mastered the art of holding an audience's interest, and Greg's continued attentiveness had her feeling a little light-headed.

"Then let's scout out a ladies' room and I'll tell you my plan." Greg nudged her forward before she had the chance to register what he was saying.

His hand hovered around the small of her back, not quite touching, yet Jackie was keenly aware of its proximity.

"You need to find the ladies' room, too?" she asked as they moved down three flights to the ground floor. Nervousness gave her the tendency to be flip.

"No. I'm sending you into the ladies' room with my shirt so you can pull yourself together minus the table-cloth." He was already unbuttoning his way down the crisp cotton of his white dress shirt. The intimate action sent a wave of unexpected longing through her.

Jackie couldn't have stopped herself from peeking if she'd tried. Too bad it was so dark in the stairwell or she would have inspected every new inch of bronzed flesh on the corporate Adonis.

His tan made her own skin look ghostly pale in comparison. And the hints of muscles in the V of that un-buttoned shirt...

Jackie swallowed.

Surely the shadows were playing tricks on her.

"What will you wear home?" she asked mostly just to distract herself from thoughts she had no business thinking.

Namely her lips tracing a path along ridges of mus-cle defining his abs.

In the middle of that image, a vision growing more explicit by the second, Jackie remembered a popular musician's myth that you couldn't create works of great passion until you lost your virginity.

A silly superstition of course. But the musician's counterpart to an old wives' tale was well known to those in the business. She'd had a fading diva for a mu-sic teacher once who'd told her she wouldn't be able to sing until she'd screwed.

Jackie had written off the bawdy advice with a laugh. Funny how that wisdom came roaring back in her ears as she stood drooling over Greg's very male physique.

What was the matter with her?

"I'm a guy. I don't need to wear a shirt home," Greg assured her. "Besides, I live two blocks from here."

Jackie shook herself to ward off a sudden onslaught of sexual images. She'd never suffered from too much drooling over any man, or really regretted her doggedly persistent virginity either, for that matter.

But the pangs of awareness shooting through her now had her wondering if maybe she'd been saving it up for a little too long.

They'd reached the bottom of the stairwell, and Greg shouldered his way through the heavy door onto the street. Darkness had fallen, but the streetlights still made it seem brighter outdoors. They stepped out into a short alleyway, a few feet from the street that ran along the front of the bar.

"No ladies' room here," Greg observed. "There must not be any access to the rest of the building from this side. Did you want to go back in the front doors?"

No. No. And hell no.

How did she get herself into these fixes? She truly did have a formidable IQ. And she had managed to ace college with a summa cum laude stamp of approval on her degree. Why did things like this always happen to her?

"No. I'll just go with the tablecloth, thanks." She wondered if she looked as ridiculous as she sounded.

Whiskers, a tail and a tablecloth. No doubt she looked *twice* as ridiculous. "I can drop it by the restaurant Monday after I have it cleaned."

A crowd of frat boys singing some college fight song stumbled out of the bar, passing the alleyway. They never noticed Jackie and Greg, but Greg stood between her and the street just in case.

She didn't know much about this guy, but she had to admit he seemed like a gentleman. She knew lots of men who would have been more than happy to let her bumble her way out of the shredded kitty suit incident without benefit of table linens. Greg had been really nice to charge to the forefront for her.

"Look, Jackie...it is Jackie, right?" He lifted one eyebrow in query.

"Jacquelyn Brady. Jackie for short." She offered her hand again, clinging to normal rules of polite society for a change. She seemed to have broken too many rules in one evening to be anything less than well bred for the rest of the night. "Nice to meet you."

"Greg De Costa." He shook her hand and flashed her a wicked grin along with a mouth full of pearly whites. "Likewise."

Was it her imagination, or did the name sound familiar? Jackie was bad with names, but she never forgot a face. And she was positive she'd never run into Greg before. She wrote off the twinge of recognition she'd felt upon hearing his last name.

"Now that we've covered the introductions, I really think I'd better go." She had auditions in the morning. She had a song to write tonight.

Mostly, she needed to escape Greg De Costa and his way too seductive chest before she did something she regretted. Like inch down her tablecloth and plaster herself to him for a good-night kiss he wouldn't soon forget.

Greg dug into his pants pocket and emerged with a cell phone as thin as a credit card. "Do me a favor and call Zing-O-Gram first to be sure Gregory doesn't get the surprise of a lifetime at his birthday party."

How could she refuse? Jackie hated to think somewhere a six-year-old boy was getting an eyeful ten years too early. Almost as bad was the thought that somewhere in Boston there was a six-year-old boy whose special surprise never arrived.

Jackie would stay with Greg just long enough to straighten out the mix-up before she went home. Then she'd put her tennis shoes in high gear so she could put some serious space between her and a slick charmer like Greg De Costa.

She needed to escape those dangerous abs.

And those sexy suspenders.

And the stupid voice in her head that kept suggesting the time had arrived to follow her old music teacher's advice and unleash the power of her singing voice.

3

GREG WATCHED JACKIE conduct her half of the phone conversation, admiring the way she could cradle the receiver, gesture wildly to express herself and still hold the tablecloth in a death grip.

How could he not admire a woman who possessed the body of a goddess *and* the ability to multitask?

He had to admit, Jackie Brady was very appealing, even if she spoke "disaster" with the fluency of a second language.

But he was only going to try and convince her to let him drive her home.

And maybe angle for a good-night kiss.

He just wanted one taste of those cat-woman lips and then he'd be able to walk away. No doubt a woman like Jackie with her penchant for trouble could have a man chasing his own damn tail in no time.

No way was Greg getting sucked into that again. He had recently dated a co-worker who thought Greg could help her advance from weather girl to head meteorologist. She'd ended up broadcasting a hurricane update with a picture of Greg's face glued in the eye of the storm and had nearly cost him his job. Then there was the lady lawyer. A safe enough choice right? She'd chased ambulances right along with Greg's camera crews, only too happy to have an "in" on late-breaking news.

So, even though Jackie happened to have the most phenomenal breasts he'd ever seen, the most tantalizing voice he'd ever heard, he didn't have any intentions of pursuing anything with her. He was swearing off women until he could get his professional life back in order. He could settle for a kiss though, couldn't he?

The door to the stairwell opened behind them just as Jackie hung up the phone. His brother stepped halfway into the alley, propping the heavy exit door with one shoulder.

"The real stripper is here," Mike announced, scarcely articulating the words around a pink rose clamped between his teeth. He shot a sheepish grin at Jackie. "No offense to you, of course, miss."

Jackie smiled right back at him, sparking a pang in Greg he could only guess was jealousy.

"None taken." She tweaked the stem of Mike's flower. "I'm glad to see Rosie is back on track at the right assignment."

"And how." Mike clutched his heart as if he'd fallen in love all over again. "Rosie's a beauty, Greg. You coming upstairs?"

"No thanks. I'm taking Jackie home." Greg knew without a doubt any other woman would pale in comparison to Jackie, no matter how many more alphabets Rosie boasted for a cup size.

Mike offered up a drunken salute while Jackie made a strangled sound and started backing away.

Greg had to jog to catch her. "Wait up, Jackie—"

She turned on him in a flurry of red hair and white linen. "Why? So you can take me *home?*" Her green eyes sparkled fire like some sort of 3D-animated video game warrior woman. "Don't men even ask permission first? Or I suppose you just assume that because I flashed you a bit more than I'd intended that I must want company for the night."

"Hey wait a minute—"

"No, you wait a minute." She pointed at him with one unadorned finger, one unpainted fingernail. "I am definitely *not* interested, so you can take your suspenders and your muscles and all the charming chat and you can find someone else to bring home with you tonight."

Greg had to remind himself he was not a fan of histrionics or furious females. For a moment, he regretted the fact because Jackie Brady definitely had a knack for the dramatic.

Although her diatribe probably fell somewhat short of her desired impact given that she was still wearing the kitty whiskers. The fuzzy ears. The pink nose painted over her own.

When she stomped off in her tennis shoes, however, Greg pulled himself together and chased after her.

Careful to keep his distance, he ran alongside her, layering on the "charming chat." He'd never had any woman refer to his blunt manner of speaking as anything remotely close to charming.

"Jackie." He waited until she shot him an evil glare. Was he so totally sick that the green daggers she shot his way turned him on? "I won't apologize for being interested, because I am."

She harrumphed and tugged her tail closer, checking the street for a cab that probably wouldn't appear at this hour.

"But I only meant to say I wanted to escort you to *your* home, to make sure you got there okay." He watched her as she thought over his words. He could practically see her recount their conversation mentally, her eyes darting across the landscape, unseeing, as she reviewed the exchange in her mind.

She slowed to a stop. "You meant you wanted to take me home...to my home?"

He halted in front of her, still careful not to crowd her. "Yes."

"So you didn't mean to imply for a minute that you were spending the night with me?"

Was it his imagination, or did she sound vaguely disappointed?

"I just don't like the idea of you wandering around the city in that torn getup all by yourself. You might attract the wrong kind of attention."

"Then I appreciate the offer." A smile spread across her whole face.

"My car is just up here on the left—"

"I never accept rides with strangers though." She rocked back and forth on the heels of her tennis shoes. "I don't know you *that* well."

"But how can I see you home if you won't let me drive you?" He looked up and down the street. "I haven't seen a cab since we left the bar."

"You uptown boys." Shaking her head in mock despair, she reached underneath the folds of her oversized toga and came up with two silver coins. Tokens in fact. "Welcome to my world, Greg. You're going to love the metro."

Great. Just great.

He'd known Jackie for all of half an hour and already she was making him revisit a past he wanted to leave far behind. How could a woman turn his life upside down so fast?

Still, he was powerless to say no. Some die-hard notion of honor told him he couldn't leave Jackie until he knew she was safe. He squeezed his eyes shut for a bracing two seconds, then plucked one token out of her hand.

He had the feeling he was in for the ride of his life.

JACKIE SWITCHED HER tail from one hand to the other, watching Greg sway along with the green line subway train. She'd secured her pants and buttoned Greg's shirt as high as it would go, but she still wore her tablecloth as a shawl for good measure. They'd already changed trains once, and now they were headed toward Jackie's apartment near Boston College.

What a night.

She couldn't believe she was being escorted home by Mr. Way Too Corporate, Greg De Costa. She still thought his name sounded familiar. Maybe she'd just read about him in the business pages of the *Globe* or something.

He looked incredibly out of place here. After he'd insisted she wear his dress shirt, he'd bought a Boston Bruins shirt for himself from a street vendor near the subway station. The black and yellow shirt made for an interesting contrast with his pleated dress pants. He'd stuffed his tie in his pants pocket.

But even with his offbeat garb, Greg managed to look worlds apart from the Friday night subway crowd. Jackie had laughed when he whipped an old-fashioned monogrammed handkerchief out of his pocket and dusted off a seat for her before she sat down.

Greg was all class and manners, the sort of man her parents would adore. The sort of man Jackie normally avoided more than tea parties.

Of course, staying away from Greg would be a lot easier if he didn't look so appealing even in the tackiest tourist T-shirt.

Jackie hugged her arms closer to her body.

"Warm enough?" Greg asked, tugging on a corner of the tablecloth.

Given the fact that she wasn't wearing a bra, Jackie had thought it would be best to keep something more than Greg's cotton dress shirt between her and the rest of the world. Just knowing that he'd worn the same shirt an hour ago over his own bare chest did shivery things to her body, especially with the woodsy notes of his cologne teasing her nose.

She nodded, her voice rusty in her throat. She could not afford to catch a chill the night before auditions. Not to mention, she kept hoping for a big callback on Monday from WBCI, Boston's biggest network affiliate station. She'd made a killer demo tape for them last week, and they were supposedly eager for new voice-over talent.

The voice-over work could be her long-awaited big break, especially given that she'd probably blown the audition for the herbal store with her impromptu jungle-themed song.

Oh well. Win some, lose some. Jackie lived by her own luck, and she had a good feeling about the network job.

"The next stop is Boston College," Greg reminded her, swiveling in his seat to catch a glimpse of the signs outside the window as flashes of light zipped past them in the darkened tunnel. "Is that where we want to get off?"

His leg brushed hers as he moved, the rattle of the train car pushing them together all the more. The summer-weight wool of his pants scratched lightly against her thigh and what remained of her fuzzy leggings. She'd tied the leftover top of her shredded costume around her waist to serve as a belt, but Jackie kept checking and rechecking the knot. It wouldn't surprise her if she lost the pants, too. It had been that kind of night.

"Yes, this is me." Jackie stood carefully, clutching a pole for support as the train's brakes hissed to a stop. "But you don't need to walk me home, Greg. I'm just glad I didn't have to ride the metro by myself like this."

He glared at her with a look that said she was being more difficult than she had any right to be, a look her parents had perfected a long time ago. Was it her fault she didn't do everything in life with perfect aplomb?

"I'm coming with you," Greg reproved her, following her off the train and into the subway station.

A lone guitarist strummed a lively tune, entertaining a small crowd who'd been waiting for the green line. As the musician lost his audience to the train Greg and Jackie had just departed, Greg tossed several bills into the guy's hat.

"That was very nice of you," Jackie whispered as they walked away across scuffed ceramic tiles. The train groaned into motion behind them, drowning out the guitar as they climbed the steps to street level.

"Subway entertaining is a tough field," Greg informed her, surprising her with his empathy for a guy who looked like he hadn't washed in several days.

Greg appeared to scope out the street scene around them, then situated himself between the traffic thoroughfare and Jackie. She wondered what he thought of her neighborhood. Did it look old to his eyes? Or were the sturdy brownstones full of character to him the way they always had been to Jackie?

He scarcely touched her as they strolled through the warm spring night, but his presence loomed all around her as he steered her around a few late-night pedestrians, nudged her forward when lights changed from "Do Not Walk" to "Walk."

"Have you ever entertained in a subway?" Jackie asked, easily slipping into "flip" mode now that she was nervous and combating attraction full steam again.

"No. But I spent a summer entertaining in a rowdy bar, so I can project those difficulties multiplied."

The battalion of flip remarks dried up on her tongue. The image of Greg as a nightclub performer didn't match her impression of him at all. Maybe he was an artist in disguise. A fact that would make a fling with him more of a real possibility.

She wouldn't risk dating some corporate yes-man who ignored his own dreams in deference to the almighty dollar, but maybe she could take a chance on an artist who supported himself with a day job.

"You? Barroom entertainment?" Some of her nervousness vanished as she reprocessed her vision of Greg De Costa. Maybe he wasn't as highbrow as she'd initially thought. Maybe he wouldn't shudder at the thought of a little adventure in life. Or misadventure, as so often was the case with Jackie.

"It was a long time ago." Greg looked up at the buildings as they trekked down Jackie's street. "What did you say your number was?"

"Three sixty-three." She didn't want to go home just yet. She was only just starting to find out the interesting stuff. "What kind of entertaining did you do?" The flip demon made a small resurgence. "Were you a stripper?"

He shook his head, but he couldn't hide the beginnings of a grin. "Hardly."

"A guitarist?"

"I played piano."

Nothing could have doused her interest faster. Both her mother and father played classical piano, touring with various philharmonics and orchestras when they weren't teaching out of their palatial Back Bay home.

Jackie played everything but the piano. Her favorite instruments were things like banjos and steel guitars. Instruments that drove her parents insane and proved to Jackie she wanted different things out of life than what they'd already achieved.

"I see." She started hunting for her building in earnest, realizing she'd been foolish to think Mr. Corporate would appreciate something outside the traditional realm. He probably had a Steinway in his living room, first class all the way.

"I take it you don't like the piano?" Greg asked, his pace slowing as they drew toward Jackie's door.

Her brownstone was the only one on the block with a burgundy-colored door and big bushes of purple heather out front. Both were her touches, little extras her elderly landlord was only too happy to receive.

The street was quiet. There wasn't much activity on Jackie's block, even on the weekends. The college students lived a few blocks over, far enough away to keep the noise level down, close enough to support lots of inexpensive restaurants and artsy pubs.

Right now, the only noise she heard was Greg's silky baritone and the soft hum of the streetlights.

She shrugged. "I like the piano."

"Let me guess, you prefer the piccolo. Or maybe a big set of cymbals." Greg stuffed his hands in his pockets and tilted one shoulder into a nearby streetlamp.

"As it happens, I love a good pair of cymbals. And I can play a mean kazoo."

"Do you always take the road less traveled, Jackie Brady?" He studied her with the aid of the streetlight, his brown eyes probing hers for answers she wasn't ready to give.

"What does it look like?" She twitched her whiskers by scrunching up her nose and maneuvering her lips.

"It looks like you're hell-bent for mayhem, lady." He lifted himself away from the lamppost and walked closer to her. Slowly. Steadily.

Her heart picked up a jaunty beat, drumming heat through her in an insistent rhythm.

Jackie was ready. Willing. Hungry for a taste of Greg.

What did it matter if he could play piano? If he lived in corporate paradise and liked to stick to the rules? Jackie could still kiss him.

She could still see where a kiss led.

She could still fantasize about losing her virginity to a man who could unlock her passionate nature and free the artist inside her.

He paused a foot in front of her, his square shoulders and tanned arms making her insides turn warm and liquid.

She was probably supposed to wait for him to kiss her, but Jackie had never been one to play by the rules.

Especially not when a risk this tempting was so close at hand.

GREG HAD EVERY INTENTION of kissing her.

He'd been dying to taste those lips ever since she'd strutted through Flanagan's in whiskers and cat ears.

He just hadn't planned on doing it so fast.

Just when he'd been sizing up the situation, taking in the details of her curves and nuances so he could wring out every possible bit of pleasure from it for both of them, Jackie dropped her tablecloth. Before he could fully appreciate the view of her braless body underneath his shirt, she plastered herself against him for the most mind-blowing kiss he'd ever experienced.

She was like a sensory explosion, swamping every inch of him with tantalizing sensations. Her lips swayed over his in slow undulations, leaving him no choice but to seek entrance to her mouth for a more thorough taste.

Sweet and complex. Jackie tasted like a dessert wine and left him hungering for more.

But all the while he tried to drink in her taste, she was tormenting his chest with the soft nudge of her breasts. No elaborate contraptions of Lycra or spandex hid her from him, only the cotton of their shirts. Taut crests peaked against him, reminding him of what she looked like naked. He could envision those breasts, those upturned nipples, perfectly.

And the memory was killing him.

"Jackie." He pulled away in slow degrees only because he had to. They were in the middle of the sidewalk for crying out loud. "Jackie?"

He kissed her one last time, or so he told himself it would be one last time, before backing up a step, still holding her hands. He wanted to go upstairs with her and unveil her body at his leisure, not maul her in full view of her neighbors.

He hadn't counted on seeing her eyes still closed, her lips still thrust forward even after his retreat.

Something inside him turned to mush at the sight. He hoped like hell it was only his brain.

"Jackie?" He squeezed her fingers in his hands.

She smiled before she opened her eyes. "Hmm?"

The sound of a window opening somewhere in the building behind them reminded Greg of their public surroundings.

Greg stepped close again, more than willing to continue this inside her apartment even if they were as compatible as oil and water. They obviously had serious chemistry going despite being as different from one another as night and day.

He always did have a hard time learning a lesson.

He could take one more chance on a woman without getting overly distracted, right? He'd go to work in the morning, listen to his desk full of demo tapes, and crawl back into bed with Jackie. A relationship didn't have to interfere with his work, damn it.

"Do you mind if I come inside?" It didn't seem like that big of an assumption in light of the kiss she'd just given him.

"What?" Her green eyes sharpened into focus immediately.

"I mean, do you want me to come upstairs with you?"

Greg was surprised to realize he was practically holding his breath. He couldn't remember the last time he'd wanted a woman this bad. Had he *ever* wanted a woman this much?

"Maybe we'd better not." The flash of innocence in her eyes as she declined sent warning bells clanging in his head.

Greg ignored them.

Jackie released his fingers, seemingly oblivious to the fact that she'd just shot him down harder than anyone else ever had.

She scooped her tablecloth off the sidewalk and wrapped it around her.

"But maybe we could see each other again?" she prompted, her throaty voice practically purring with feminine satisfaction.

She wanted to see him again.

His breath returned, clearing his head in time for him to form a response.

"How about next weekend?" He had to be careful not to ask her out for tomorrow. As much as he wanted Jackie, he could not afford to let any woman twist his life around and make him forget his priorities. Not now when he finally had the world by the tail.

Tail.

His eyes dropped to Jackie's feline accoutrements, amazed how his every thought already twined with images of her.

"Sounds good." She nodded, a small smile curling her perfect lips.

He couldn't be sure in the dim light, but he thought maybe she blushed.

Digging in his wallet for his business cards, he thought maybe she was just an old-fashioned girl. He'd heard they still existed. Women who didn't sleep with someone on the first date. Women who still blushed.

Greg definitely approved. He just hadn't pegged outrageous cat woman Jackie as one of those women.

He scribbled down her number on the back of one card and gave her another one in case she needed to reach him.

Who knew? Maybe she'd change her mind midweek and decide she couldn't wait for the weekend.

Fat chance.

Greg had the feeling he'd lucked into meeting a woman who would be well worth a little time away from the office. A woman who wasn't into playing games—despite the fact that she favored painting her nose pink and strutting through town wearing cat's ears.

"You're okay from here then?" Greg asked, not wanting to lose gentlemanly points this late into their evening together.

"I'm okay from here." She backed toward her front steps, smiling.

No repeat good-night kiss. Greg couldn't help the surge of disappointment. He'd been hoping maybe there'd be one more kiss to seal the deal.

Still, he wanted to roar with satisfaction that there would be more kisses, and who knew what else, in store. He had the feeling he'd have a hard time concentrating on his demo tape review tomorrow after the way she'd just set his veins on fire. But he only had a week to go to see her again.

Until then, he planned to stock up on dessert wine.

FROM THE SAFETY OF HER building's well-lit foyer, Jackie tracked Greg's progress down her street until she couldn't see him anymore.

She'd made a date with Mr. Corporate and she was feeling pretty damn giddy about it. The memory of his touch would taunt her until next weekend.

She looked down at the business card in her hands, scarcely daring to believe her good luck. Flipping it over, she read the words printed there.

Greg De Costa. General Manager.

WBCI, Channel Twelve.

The card wavered in her suddenly trembling hand. *Oh no.*

Jackie watched her fledgling career crash and burn right before her eyes.

Her bachelor party hero had turned out to be more than a ritzy member of Boston's business elite. No, that would have been far too tame for her. She'd flashed her breasts at the man who held her professional future in his hands—the veritable god of the commercial jingle world, the Zeus of recording contracts in Boston.

No wonder his name had sounded so familiar to her. Jackie had just mailed him a copy of her demo last week.

Before she'd fawned all over him.

Before she'd fallen out of her kitty costume and shown him more than any man had ever seen.

Before she'd totally blown her credibility as a serious commercial talent.

What was he going to think when he opened her application materials and discovered her name on a new demo? He was going to think what any man would think—that Jackie had gone out of her way to put herself in his path today. That she'd put on a show for him to help land a job.

Maybe she hadn't been so lucky tonight after all.

Jackie squeezed her eyes shut, knowing she was going to have to do some serious tap dancing to maneuver her way around this disaster. But after failing at one career—her cherished dream of composing more complex music—Jackie refused to screw up another.

Later, she'd figure how she could still land the voice-over slot without looking like she'd manipulated Greg.

But first things first. She didn't stand a shot in hell at that job if Greg unearthed her tape now. Before she did anything else, she needed to make a trip to WBCI to get her demo back.

Good thing Jackie was used to turning heads and causing a commotion. She had the feeling she'd have to do a little of both if she wanted to straighten out this mess.

4

WBCI SAT ON THE outskirts of Boston, a high-tech television studio in a less than stellar part of town.

Greg didn't mind the long commute. His car had state-of-the-art German engineering to smooth the back roads full of potholes, and today, he had a gorgeous woman on his mind to occupy his thoughts.

What he didn't have was a new voice-over talent for the station.

That failing clouded his mood as he pulled into his primo reserved parking space in front of the building. He hefted his briefcase out of the car, the dozens of nixed demo tapes inside adding considerably to its weight.

What he hadn't heard on any of these demo tapes was a voice like Jackie Brady's. Had his listening ear been prejudiced after the sweet seduction of her perfect pitch? Or had there genuinely been no good candidates for the station's in-house voice-over vacancy?

He mulled over the question on the way to his office. The penthouse in this relatively short building was only on the sixth floor, but it didn't matter to Greg, who preferred to spend time getting work done as opposed to gazing out the window.

Of course, no matter how much Jackie's singing

voice haunted his dreams and possibly biased his professional opinions, Greg had to be grateful there was no chance they would ever be working together. He'd seen firsthand how detrimental a personal relationship could be to a professional one. Ever since the meteorologist incident, Greg made sure not to mingle his personal and professional lives.

Therefore, no matter how much he kept thinking Jackie would be a great voice-over talent, he counted his blessings she was safely involved in another career. He would keep her and her cat whiskers in his private life and figure out another way to solve his station's dilemma.

Exiting the elevator into the sixth-floor lobby, Greg sensed trouble brewing. More than half the seats in the small reception area were occupied by WBCI employees. Every single one of those employees looked up expectantly as he sought his office.

He almost had the door unlocked when the barrage of questions began. Ten seconds later he was swarmed.

The engineer from the editing room pushed her way to the front of the pack. She was poker buddies with the lady meteorologist who'd caused Greg so much grief and she didn't waste any opportunity to give him a hard time. "Greg, I've got to polish up the department store commercials this week to show the client. Any word on an in-house person for the voice-over, or do you want me to freelance it out?"

"Same here, Greg," called one of his right-hand producers from the back of the crowd. "I need a voice for the Pink Lady Club and you told me you didn't want one of our news anchors to fill in for a risqué spot like that. Didn't you say you'd have some talent contracted by today?"

Greg worked the lock behind his back while he doled out smooth assurances. "I've just got to iron out the contract details." As the lock gave, he backed his way into his private offices. "Give me a couple of hours to nail things down and I'll have a name for you this afternoon."

He hoped.

Assuming he could put Jackie's voice behind him for a few hours and concentrate on the few remaining tapes that might have filtered their way onto his desk over the weekend. If that didn't work, he'd dig through the pile of demos in his briefcase all over again until he found the right sound.

Tossing his keys across the desk and stabbing a few computer keys, Greg assured himself he could do this.

He just needed total focus and concentration.

What he didn't need was a body lying on his camel-colored leather office couch.

Holy...

"Hey, Greg." His brother Mike rose out of the tangled chenille throw blanket and a rumpled dinner jacket he had obviously tossed over his body, then propped himself up on an elbow. "Hope you don't mind I crashed here last night."

Greg dropped his briefcase to the floor with a thud. "How did you get in?"

"You gave me a backup key when you took this job, remember?" Mike shrugged, the casual gesture belying his shell-shocked expression. "I hope it wasn't a big deal. Hannah dumped me last night and I—didn't feel like going home."

Son of a...

Greg sank into his oversized leather office chair, allowing the news to roll over him. "What do you mean she dumped you? You're getting married."

"I guess one of the waitresses at Flanagan's used to work in the cafeteria where Hannah teaches school. Hannah got wind of the naked women at the bachelor party and she lost it. Told me I've only got eyes for other women—Jesus, Greg, you know that's not true."

"Yeah *I* know, but how the hell does Hannah know? You've got a tendency to lay on the charm with females." Mike had a reputation that went back to high school.

"I'm a gentleman, damn it. That's why I'm nice to women in general. That's why I don't—indulge myself—with my future wife. I'm showing her some respect." Mike tugged down his shirt cuffs to straighten his sleeves, not making eye contact.

Poor bastard. Greg suspected his brother was hurting like hell over this.

Greg didn't know how he was going to juggle finding a voice-over talent, shoving Jackie out of his thoughts and talking his brother through this new crisis, but he'd find a way. He felt partly responsible since he'd let Mike's friends talk him into hiring a stripper for the bachelor party anyway. And then there was Jackie, who definitely possessed the power to distract the most stalwart of faithful men.

Taking a deep breath, Greg scanned his brain for options.

And came up with only one. He had no choice but to multitask.

"Then I guess we'd better figure out a way for you to convince Hannah you're not ogling other women on the sly. But I'm going to have to sift through these tapes while we talk." Greg nodded toward the coffeemaker as he started tearing into the oversized manila envelopes on his desk that might contain the voice he was looking for. "You make the java while I get a start on these and then we'll figure out how you can win Hannah back."

Preferably before Mike's wedding in less than three weeks.

Hell, preferably before noon.

Greg had a job to maintain and a studio to run. And no reprobate brother or pseudo-stripper with cat whiskers was going to make him forget it.

SHE SHOULD HAVE WORN HER whiskers.

Jackie regretted her boring but professional navy-blue suit as soon as she walked through the tinted glass doors of WBCI. Today's mission was too important to her career to take any chances—important enough to warrant a personal day from her copywriting job—and she'd agonized over her approach for hours.

At least when she wore the whiskers, people backed up a step when they saw her coming. She could probably sing and dance her way right into the studios, filch her demo tape from wherever the mailroom had it tucked away, and be back home by lunchtime if she had the distraction factor of a cat suit.

Now, she had no choice but to stick with her more conservative plan—wheedle the tape out of the receptionist before Greg discovered it this morning.

Self-consciously patting her semicontrolled hairdo, Jackie got directions to the sixth-floor lobby from the main receptionist. She clicked her way up the stairwell to buy herself a little more pep talk time.

Besides, sticking to the paths less traveled meant less likelihood of bumping into Greg—a disaster she couldn't begin to imagine.

Forcing her thoughts back to the pep talk, Jackie guessed her tape would have only arrived at the network this weekend. She'd been nearing the deadline for applying to the voice-over position when she'd dropped her package in the mail, so she'd taken careful note of the dates.

With any luck, the demo tapes were collecting in the mailroom until Greg was ready to review them. It shouldn't be any trouble for an administrative type person to hand Jackie back her envelope with the help of the great cover story she'd come up with.

Okay, the almost believable cover story she'd settled on after racking her brain for hours.

Pausing outside the metal door painted with an oversized 6, Jackie centered herself with a grounding note, humming out a rich, round middle C to clear her head. She staunchly ignored enticing images of Greg De Costa in burgundy suspenders and armed with a tablecloth.

If she wanted this mission to succeed, damn it, she couldn't afford to think about him.

She could save her career *and* a possible future date with Greg simply by waltzing in there and snagging her demo right now.

As long as she didn't happen to run into him and his too sexy for his own good self.

With the stage presence she'd cultivated at an early age, Jackie blasted through the metal door and left most of her thoughts of Mr. Suspenders in the stairwell. She flashed her best smile at the receptionist in the lobby, praying the door right behind the young man didn't read "Gregory De Costa" the way she damn well knew it did.

At least the receptionist was a guy. She'd caught one break today.

"Can I help you?" The broad-shouldered blond behind the small desk stood, giving Jackie a better view of *his* suspenders—yellow-and-green striped decorated with tiny shamrocks.

"Oh yes, I certainly hope so." She also hoped her attempts at wide-eyed innocence looked convincing and not like she'd just had a facelift. "You'll never believe the terrible mistake I've made..."

She launched into her convoluted tale about a magnet sitting next to her demo tapes while they were in her Jeep—not that she had a Jeep of course, but she rather thought the car worked with the cover story—and inadvertently erasing all the audio off the cassettes.

The administrative assistant who'd introduced himself as Chip furrowed a blond brow. "I thought magnets only affected videotapes that way?"

Did they? Jackie had no clue. "Me too! That's why I didn't worry about that magnet on the passenger seat. Anyway, would it be too much trouble to..."

Was that music she heard emanating from behind Chip?

"I wondered if maybe you could give me my application package back," she continued, distracted by strains of a jazz song coming from Greg's office.

A jazz song she'd put on her demo tape to showcase her range of vocal talent.

Horror immobilized her, gluing her navy-blue pumps to the Persian carpet.

"I guess I can go see if Mr. De Costa has the tape in his stack," Chip offered, jolting Jackie out of deep-freeze mode as he backed toward the big door marked "General Manager."

"No!" She flew around his desk to plant herself between him and Greg's door.

He stared at her like she'd just lost her mind. Which she most definitely had.

If ever a situation had warranted a song and dance routine, this was it.

"I, um, didn't realize you'd have to bother your boss." She held off Chip with some manic eyelash batting that probably looked more like nervous twitching than flirtation. Which, of course, it was.

The strains of her jazz selection faded away in the background. She didn't have to listen to know her improvised bubble gum commercial would be up next.

Assuming Greg didn't wing her tape into the trash can when he saw her name on her application.

"It's no trouble," Chip assured her, frowning. "But if you insist—"

"I insist." What else could she do? She'd been five minutes too late to save herself a lot of embarrassment. The only thing left for her to do was sneak out while her future in network television went up in flames.

She had only retreated a step when the door to the general manager's office came flying open, the bubble gum commercial amplified.

"Where in the hell did we get this?" Greg De Costa stood framed in the doorway, his blue-and-yellow striped tie contrasting with all blue suspenders. Shirtsleeves rolled to his elbows, he carried a manila envelope in his hand along with a couple of sheets of paper.

For a split second, his gaze focused on Chip. Obviously, Greg's assistant had been the anticipated recipient of his question.

Screw the navy pumps, Jackie attempted a sideways shuffle step to exit this outrageous scene.

Too bad she didn't move two feet away before Greg's dark-brown gaze landed on her.

"You." He didn't point a finger at her, but his lone word had the same effect.

"Hi, Greg." She forced a smile as the bubble gum commercial gave way to a more adult-oriented advertisement for a regional prophylactics manufacturer. "There is really a crazy explanation for this."

Greg opened his mouth to speak until Jackie's taped voice filtered through the outer lobby, promising enhanced sensual pleasure to the man who used the thinnest prophylactic product on the market.

His mouth snapped shut, leaving Jackie to weather the awkward conversational moment. She'd never been embarrassed of that commercial before, but then, she'd never had to listen to it in front of a prospective employer who'd also happened to have seen her naked.

Refusing to give in to self-consciousness now, Jackie used the time to launch into her explanation. "I guess I didn't mention the other night that I'm not just a Zing-O-Gram girl."

Greg's eyes nearly crossed during the breathy final words of the condom ad. Something about finding your own pleasure—tonight.

Maybe her demo tape would win him over to her talent for voice-overs after all.

Chip edged his way closer. "You're a Zing-O-Gram girl, too?"

Jackie couldn't help but smile despite the hideous circumstances of the day.

Chip would have loved the cat costume.

BY THE TIME GREG SNAPPED out of the sexual spell Jackie's voice had cast over him with the condom ad, he realized she was knee deep in causing a commotion again.

His administrative assistant was hitting on her, every man within spitting distance of the lobby had ceased working to listen to the suggestive demo tape advertisement, and—what the?—Jackie was currently demonstrating tap dance moves to an enthralled Chip.

"Why don't we discuss this in private?" Greg slid a hand around her elbow to hustle her into his office. Hadn't he promised himself there would be no more big scenes in his life in the wake of the meteorologist fiasco?

He edged her away from the lobby full of prying eyes and into his office with only one set of prying eyes.

"Hi, Mike." Jackie winked at Greg's brother, politely ignoring the fact that Mike reclined on the office couch like a permanent fixture, the chenille throw still tucked around him, coffee in hand.

"Hey, beautiful." Mike smiled for the first time all morning. "The demo is unbelievable."

Greg jerked a thumb toward the door. "Mike, you're going to have to go get breakfast or something. Jackie, why don't you have a seat?"

She tilted her chin and didn't budge while Mike sped for the door and closed it behind him.

"Why? Are you granting me an interview for the voice-over talent?"

Despite the unapologetic determination in Jackie's eyes, Greg would swear she looked just a little bit hopeful.

She also looked every inch the professional in her navy-blue suit and her I-mean-business heels. Only her cinnamon-colored curls springing free of a restraining clip at the back of her neck gave any indication of Jackie's wild side.

Damn it, he would have hired her in a minute if she hadn't resorted to the stripper stunt to get his attention.

Sighing, he backed up a step to escape the allure of simple scents surrounding her, the coconut fragrance of her shampoo, the peppermint of her chewing gum, the vaguely citrusy notes that emanated from her body....

"I *can't* give you an interview, Jackie." He stressed the words for his benefit as much as hers. To put a little more space between them, he wandered over to the playback deck and pressed stop to halt her demo. "How can we ever work together after kicking off a professional relationship with a striptease?"

Unbidden, the image of her bared breasts invaded his brain.

Jackie's cheeks turned pink, but that didn't diminish the scowl she sent his way. "That was an accident. I had no idea you'd be at the party the other night, and I certainly didn't mean to flash you so much..." her cheeks flushed all the darker "...skin."

"Didn't you?" He hated to call her on the carpet here, but what was he supposed to think when her demo tape showed up on his desk right after her cat woman seduction?

"No, I most certainly didn't." She took a step closer. The voice she wielded so skillfully on the demo tape now turned noticeably icy. "I've never been so embarrassed in all my life, if you must know the truth, but I thought your gallant attempt to help me out of an awkward situation meant you understood that." She stood toe to toe with him, anger radiating from her like a fever. "Apparently I was wrong."

She spun on her heel, her slim pantsuit accentuating every twitch of her retreating hips.

Damn. What if *he'd* been wrong?

"Jackie, wait." Maybe she deserved an explanation too. Especially on the off chance she was telling him the truth. "Even if I am jumping to conclusions here—"

"You are." She folded her arms in the classic skeptic's stance, but waited for him to continue.

"—I still can't hire you after the way we first met." He'd be consigning himself to sure disaster. "I've had personal relationships with women I've met through the studio before, and it just makes things awkward."

Her shoulders relaxed just a little. "Work is everything to me, too. If you hire me, we obviously won't pursue a personal relationship. I'm fine with that."

Did she have to sound so eager to comply? Greg already hated the idea of not seeing her again.

"But could we really get past our first meeting?" How would he work with her after the dreams he'd had about her all weekend? He wasn't about to sacrifice his professional capabilities every damn time they needed to record a condom ad.

"We're both adults, Greg. I don't think it will be a problem." She stepped closer.

Desperation clawed at him as the scent of her chewing gum wafted his way again. He'd never been so hungry for the taste of peppermint in all his life.

"It's a problem for *me*, Jackie. I tangled with the studio weathergirl once and my career—my standing at the station, anyway—really took a hit. I don't want to end up in that position again."

He steeled himself against the disappointment in her eyes, the deflated sag of her shoulders. Even her cinnamon curls looked a little less springy.

But she shook it off so fast, Greg wondered if maybe he'd only dreamed the momentary lapse. She sauntered over to the playback deck against one wall of his office and popped her tape out of the receiver. "Then that's your loss, Greg, because I would have been the best talent this studio has ever seen."

No kidding. And now it was almost noon and Greg had no one to fill the slot that sorely needed a stellar voice.

"You've got great pipes. I'll give you that." She had great everything else too, but there was no sense going there.

"You sure you don't want to change your mind?" She dropped the tape into an oversized brown leather purse. "I can quit my day job *and* the Zing-O-Gram business in about five seconds and be to work in ten."

Temptation pulled at him, made him question his decision. Memories of the weathergirl using a red X taped over his face during the hurricane forecast on network television wouldn't let him be swayed.

"Sorry, Jackie. There's just no way I can work with you and still hang on to my job and my sanity."

"I guess I have no choice but to respect that." She nodded, accepting a situation that had to have negative implications for her. Even if she had maneuvered her way into the pseudo-stripper stunt last Friday, maybe it only meant she really needed the voice-over job. "But I can't imagine we'll be ready to see one another on a personal level after this either."

Damn. This was definitely *not* how he wanted things to shake down. But sometimes good negotiations were all about compromise.

"Sorry about our date," he agreed for now, hoping once this morning's debacle passed, she'd feel differently. He would call her later. Apologize profusely. Convince her to still see him this weekend.

He extended his hand in an attempt to soothe over any bad feeling between them, but Jackie's cell phone rang before they could say goodbye.

Greg took the opportunity to retrieve her manila envelope and her application papers for her from Chip's desk. By the time he returned to his office, Jackie was just putting away her phone.

Was it his imagination, or was she trying to suppress a grin?

"That was an herbal store I auditioned for last week," Jackie explained. "They're hiring me for a national spot for their chain of stores that's going to be filmed right here in Boston."

A warning bell started blaring somewhere in the back of Greg's mind. He'd personally signed on an herbal store franchise account two weeks ago.

The warning bell muted into the dangerous-as-hell lure of Jackie's siren voice.

"In fact, the Back To Nature stores are doing their taping at WBCI right under your nose, Greg." She smiled as she took her application papers out of his hands. "Despite your best effort, it looks like we're going to be working together after all."

As she sailed out of his office, head held high, Greg realized she didn't need the benefit of a white tablecloth cape flapping in her wake.

Even in conservative pumps and a pantsuit, Jackie Brady knew how to make a hell of an exit.

5

IN YOUR FACE, Greg De Costa.

Jackie did a mental victory dance as she closed the door to the general manager's office behind her. Sure she might have lost out on a huge break when Greg refused to give her a shot at the voice-over position, but she'd just gained a fantastic career opportunity with a big-budget, high-visibility television commercial.

And by God, she'd show the man just how much he'd lost out when he passed her over. Personally *and* professionally.

She understood why he hadn't offered her the job, even though she didn't like it. But it rankled a bit that he'd given up on their date so easily.

Jackie refused to think about what might have been. She'd been subjected to enough rigid attitudes in her lifetime thanks to her parents. She didn't need a man in her life who couldn't get past her cat suit falling off when they'd first met. Why should she be penalized for faulty stitching? She'd hit her note, hadn't she?

"Have a good day, Miss Brady," Chip, the Greg-in-training administrative assistant, called to her as she walked by his desk.

She flashed him a little wave and tried not to notice

his suspenders. That particular male accoutrement would forever remind her of Greg.

Hurrying toward the stairwell door, Jackie couldn't wait to get outside the building and celebrate her new commercial. Because she *was* happy, damn it. No matter that she'd just lost a date with the hottest guy she'd ever met, this had been a *good* day.

She also needed to call the marketing firm she did freelance copywriting for and let them know she'd be unavailable for the week.

Before she reached the stairs, however, a petite blonde with long braids and a denim jumper stepped in her path.

Jackie had her pegged for a kindergarten teacher in two seconds flat even before she saw the little red schoolhouse quilted on the woman's dress pocket.

"Excuse me." The woman tossed one long braid over her shoulder and eyed Chip from the safety of a potted forsythia. "I happened to notice you just came from the general manager's office. Could you tell me if Michael De Costa is in there?"

"Not anymore." In an effort to move by the woman, Jackie reached for the stairwell door.

"Wait a minute." The pretty, delicate-looking blonde grabbed Jackie's forearm with both hands. "You mean he was in there at some point?"

Jackie frowned at the woman's urgent touch, the desperate look in her eyes. Mike De Costa was no Greg, but he was certainly a charmer in his own right. What if he had a dangerous female stalker on his tail who favored denim jumpers? Maybe Jackie shouldn't be giving the woman any information.

"He left quite some time ago," Jackie lied smoothly as she attempted to pull her arm away from the stalker kindergarten teacher's grasp.

"But he was definitely there earlier?" the woman clarified.

Jackie hoped she hadn't given away too much already. But at this point, she didn't think Miss Blond Braid would let her go if she didn't admit to seeing Mike.

"Yes, he was."

The woman released Jackie immediately, her shoulders slumping. "Thank God."

The intensity of her reaction—which was now quite obviously relief—touched Jackie. Maybe the blonde wasn't a stalker after all.

"Are you friends with Mike?" Jackie had to ask. And heaven knew, no one had ever accused her of being subtle.

Offering a halfhearted smile, the woman extended her hand. "I'm Hannah Williams, Mike's fiancée." A stricken look crossed her features. "Former fiancée."

Jackie shook her hand, not quite sure what to say beyond, "Jackie Brady. Nice to meet you."

Darn it. Her mother would know exactly what Emily Post would dictate for this awkward social moment, but Jackie floundered.

"I'm sure Mike still thinks he's engaged," Jackie assured her, stepping deeper into the corridor away from

Chip's curious gaze. "He just had a bachelor party the other night."

Hannah shook her head, blue eyes dark with unshed tears. "We broke up yesterday."

Oh.

Jackie thought about offering a "nice to meet you, have to be going" sort of sentiment and leaving Hannah to her own devices. But wouldn't that seem horribly unfeeling to a woman who'd obviously just had her heart trounced by an "I'm too professional to be personal" De Costa male?

"I'm sure it's just last-minute wedding jitters." Jackie figured her parking lot victory whoop could wait. Hannah Williams looked like she needed a shoulder to cry on.

"I doubt it. Mike has seemed preoccupied for a while—" Hannah began, then straightened as she turned a suspicious eye on Jackie. "How did *you* know about the bachelor party?"

"There was a Zing-O-Gram mix-up and I ended up performing a birthday song instead of a striptease." Did that sound as convoluted to Hannah as it did to her? "Actually, my act practically turned into a striptease when—"

Jackie stopped midsentence, realizing that Mike's fiancée might not want to know the details of any stripping scenarios. She thunked herself on the head, wishing she hadn't let her mouth run away from her.

Hannah gasped.

Pointed a pale finger at Jackie.

"You're the cat woman!"

Judging from the mild horror in Hannah's expression, Jackie guessed that wasn't a good thing. Nevertheless, she couldn't lie.

"Guilty. It was the most embarrassing moment of my entire life." Although if the crowded Flanagan's backroom had contained only Greg De Costa, the moment might have been the most arousing. "Did Mike tell you about the mistake?"

Hannah's mouth tightened into a little circle of disapproval. She looked Jackie up and down as if envisioning the scene in detail.

"No, he didn't tell me about it. That's why I blew a gasket when I learned his bachelor party had not one, but *two* strippers tearing their clothes off for Mike. I don't mind the whole exotic dancing thing, but I have a big problem with him picking and choosing what he decides to share with me."

Okay. Now she was knee deep in a domestic quarrel thanks to her decision not to walk away. Maybe her mother's insistence on following Emily Post wasn't such a bad idea.

Jackie worked on her sidestep shuffle toward the stairwell. "I can certainly see where that would be frustrating. Nice meeting you, Hannah, but I really do need to be going."

"Wait a minute." Hannah seized her in the pseudo-stalker grip again. This time, her blue eyes glittered with a new light. "I have an idea."

Far be it for Jackie to stand in the way of a madwoman's schemes. Curious, she waited.

"A cat-suit-wearing stripper is certainly familiar

with plenty of ways to add sparks to a relationship."
Hannah smiled a wicked little grin. "I need you to
teach me everything you know."

"But I'm not a stripper—"

"Okay, exotic dancer. Whatever. Works for my pur-
poses." Hannah whipped a business card out of the
pocket of her jean jumper and stuffed it in Jackie's
hand. "Here's my number. I need to get back to work,
but call me later and we'll set something up. I've got a
trust fund, so don't worry, I can definitely afford it.
We'll put you on retainer or whatever until I pick up a
few moves I can use, okay?"

Things were definitely spiraling out of control.
"Hannah, I'm not even—"

Hannah flung her arms around Jackie with all the
fervor of a long-lost sister. "You've turned my whole
day around. Thanks."

And just like that, Hannah Williams shoved through
the stairwell door and pounded her way down the
staircase in her Birkenstocks.

Jackie studied the woman's calling card with the ap-
ple and ruler border—Hannah Williams, Kindergarten
Teacher, Public School 113.

Well, didn't that beat all. Through no fault of her
own, somehow Jackie the Virgin had signed on to teach
Hannah the Kindergarten Teacher how to attract a
man.

Via striptease no less.

Of course, Jackie had been toying with the idea of
shedding her virginity anyway if she wanted to take
her career up a notch. The old musical superstition of

needing to experience passion before you could truly sing about it still niggled at her. Maybe she and Hannah could help one another form a game plan for seducing the De Costa men.

And wouldn't that just serve Greg right?

Smiling, Jackie followed Hannah down the stairs at a more leisurely pace, anticipating the fun of riling up Mr. Rigid Attitude.

Greg was about to learn the perils of underestimating Jackie Brady.

GREG NEVER UNDERESTIMATED the power of Studio A.

At least not this week.

Jackie Brady had been working on the new Back To Nature commercial inside WBCI's biggest studio for the past two days, and somehow, Greg had managed to avoid her.

Not any longer.

He stood outside the soundproof door and steeled himself for the inevitable assault to his senses the woman provided. His dreams had been saturated with the fragrance of peppermint gum and citrusy perfume, his brainwaves short-circuited by images of a singing feline in high-tops with wild, cinnamon-colored hair.

But he couldn't think about any of that right now, not when the client had requested Greg's presence in this morning's creative meeting before shooting commenced. The Back To Nature advertising budget was huge, and Greg had personally secured the account himself. He would make sure he did whatever it took to keep the client happy.

Even if it meant facing Jackie Brady again.

Greg shouldered his way through the door, his eyes adjusting to the shadowed periphery of the brightly lit, empty set in the middle of the room.

He heard Shamus Fletcher, Back To Nature's CEO, before he saw him.

"Glad you could make it, son," the scratchy, booming bass voice echoed through the high-ceilinged studio as a dark shape lumbered toward Greg. "You've got to descend that corporate ivory tower of yours every now and then."

Shamus clapped Greg on the shoulder with the force of a football coach. At six foot two, he was no taller than Greg but twice as wide. He bore such a resemblance to the Skipper on *Gilligan's Island* that Greg found himself humming the show's theme song for days after any meeting with the man. Shamus Fletcher was no bumbling sea captain, however, and had bought out Back To Nature five years ago after semi-retiring from the canned food industry. Shamus loved herbal products because, according to him, they'd improved his failing health one hundred percent.

"Nice to see you, Shamus. Your set looks great." Greg took in the soothing backdrop of blue sky and white clouds, the sedate garden setting that gave a calming visual aid to the "back to nature" theme.

Briefly, Greg wondered what role Jackie played in this tranquil world, then recalled his effort not to think about her while at work.

"I hate the set, Greg," Shamus announced, drawing Greg closer to the offending blue backdrop and effectively putting thoughts of Jackie on the back burner for at least a couple of minutes. "That's why I called the creative powwow this morning."

Greg scrambled to anticipate the man's needs. Shamus had a reputation for being an unconventional businessman, but he had the financial muscle to be as difficult as he pleased. "You think it's not realistic enough? I could get our designers in here and we could—"

Whatever he might have said evaporated from his lips as Jackie Brady waltzed into the sedate garden setting in a buff-colored suede bikini. At first glance, she didn't look like she was wearing a damn thing.

Even at second glance, she looked like she needed a tablecloth to shield her from the prying eyes of the camera crew and the set designers.

And just like that, Jackie removed herself from the back burner and switched the heat to "high."

Shamus turned to see the source of Greg's sudden preoccupation. He whistled his approval in a way that grated along Greg's every last overheated nerve.

"Now *this* is what we should be going for," Shamus practically shouted with hearty approval.

Greg tugged at his collar. "Sex?"

Shamus roared his laughter. "No, son. We should be going for wild and untamed." He gestured toward Jackie as if to illustrate the concepts. "I suggest we do more of a Tarzan-Jane jungle setup and make nature a bit edgier. What do you think?"

Greg wasn't entirely sure he still *could* think.

He struggled to tear his eyes off of Jackie's half-naked body in an effort to recover.

And then she winked at him.

Frustration fueled his thoughts even as lust still rode him. Hard.

"I think it sounds great," Greg managed, his voice a bit ragged. He cleared his throat. "We could alter the copy a bit. Maybe something along the lines of 'follow your natural instincts.'"

"Brilliant!" Shamus rewarded him with another slap on the back.

Even Jackie looked vaguely impressed as she pulled on an oversized man's chambray shirt to cover her bikini. Her legs remained bare to distract him, however.

Shamus pointed an accusing finger at Greg. "That's why you ought to be down here in the trenches, son. You're too damn valuable on the production side to be wasting your talents in the general manager's office. I'm voting you in as my producer of choice for this segment."

Shock delayed Greg's reaction.

Wasting his talents in the highest office of the local network? "Shamus, I've given you our star producer. Bill Jeffries is a top-notch—"

"But I want 'follow your natural instincts.' And I want *you*. You sold me on making this commercial locally and now I want you to stand by all that schmoozing. I want you in charge down here."

Damn. There weren't very many people who could make that sort of demand of Greg, but Shamus Fletcher was one of them. Despite the man's affability and his resemblance to the Skipper, he could buy and sell WBCI five times over with his varied financial interests. Back To Nature alone was poised for monumental market explosion.

Frankly, Greg couldn't afford to say no.

Even with the threat of Jackie Brady in a bikini hanging over his head.

Greg braved a quick glance in her direction. She stared back at him with undisguised curiosity. And, blast the woman, more than a little amusement.

She hitched at the strap of her suede bathing suit/ Jane getup through the chambray material of her shirt. The gesture shifted her curves in a way that drew the eye and made him remember exactly what she looked like naked.

And from the twinkle in her green eyes, Greg had the distinct impression Jackie was going to make the next few days pure torture for him.

COULD JACKIE HELP IT IF she was enjoying a little bit of poetic justice?

Greg hadn't hired her because he didn't want all that sexual tension zinging around in a professional environment. Now he didn't have any choice but to work with her.

Finally, he heaved out a sigh. "I can't promise eight-hour days, Shamus. I still have a station to run outside the studio."

The client tossed his head back and laughed. Old Shamus was a good sort. He probably had more money than Croesus but he wasn't nearly as uptight as Jackie's parents.

And he obviously had enough clout to make even high and mighty Greg De Costa bend to his will. The realization made Jackie all the more determined to impress Shamus, who hadn't been afraid to take a chance on her.

"I'm sure we can work around your schedule," Shamus assured Greg as he pulled on a windbreaker with a logo of a tree stitched on the breast pocket. "I've really got to run to another appointment, but I feel confident Back To Nature is in good hands now that you're on the scene."

He clapped Jackie on the shoulder hard enough that she stepped forward, propelled into Greg's personal space. They didn't touch, but she hovered close enough to absorb the light warmth of his body, to breathe the musky scent of his aftershave.

Greg's gaze met hers for one electric moment before he turned back to a retreating Shamus. "But what about the creative meeting? Don't we want to redesign the set?"

"Jackie knows what I want," he called back as he settled a baseball cap over his wispy white hair. "You two 'follow your natural instincts' and we'll be in great shape!"

The client's wicked laughter echoed through the studio even after the heavy metal door clanged shut behind him.

Uh-oh.

She'd wanted to tease Greg a little bit. She hadn't

wanted to be left alone with him where she could possibly get a taste of her own medicine.

Jackie took one look at Greg in his navy dress shirt with yellow-striped suspenders and knew she couldn't tempt him too much without tempting herself right along with him. And every time she was near Greg De Costa she automatically thought about her professional need as a singer to lose her virginity.

Well, her semiprofessional need.

Wanting to lose it to Greg in particular was probably somewhat personal.

"This is going to present a problem," Greg started, backing away from her slowly. "But we'll work around it."

"This is not going to present a problem," Jackie countered, doing a little backing up of her own. Their footwork couldn't have been any more intricate if they'd been circling one another in the boxing ring. "Because we won't let it."

She released her grip on the chambray shirt to point a stern finger in his face. "This job is more important to me than anything, and I intend to impress Shamus with my vocal abilities. Whatever history you and I might have going here is irrelevant."

Greg saluted her. "Agreed."

"Great."

"Fine." Greg grit his teeth, the muscles in his jaw flexing and relaxing in rapid-fire succession. "And since we're on the same page here, would you mind doing something to close that shirt of yours again? The buttons serve a purpose, you know."

She couldn't help the smile that tugged at her lips. She would take a lot more joy from his torment, however, if she didn't need his help dazzling the herbal store client.

"I'll button, but you've got to figure out how to make this garden-party set into a jungle by tomorrow." She wandered over to the fake bushes and the neatly laid out herbal garden. "I'm not leaving until I'm certain it looks just like Shamus and I discussed."

As she finished with the last button, she bent to move the fake bushes out of the way.

A strangled sound escaped Greg.

"What?" She set the rhododendron back on the floor.

"Pants," he rasped out like a man who's been laid up with strep throat. "Is it too much to ask for you to wear pants, too?"

Sighing, Jackie marched over to her gym bag with her extra accessories and tugged on a pair of sweats she used for dance class. "I mean it, Greg. I'm only going to humor this 'we have a history' thing so far. Get over it."

She said the words a bit more forcefully than she'd intended, but then, she'd meant the words to penetrate *her* brain as much as his. The longer she lingered in Greg's presence, the more inventive ways she came up with to use the man's suspenders.

Tying his hands to her bedposts topped the list, and *that* particular image was pretty damn distracting.

He held his hands up in mock surrender, not realizing how perfectly it played into the bedpost fantasy currently playing out in her mind.

"You're right." His hands fell back to his sides and he moved to haul the rhododendrons off the set. "I've got no business thinking of you in any way but as a fellow professional."

"Exactly." Now clothed from her toes to her neck, Jackie helped Greg disassemble the set. "And as one professional to another, Greg, I'm going to be candid about your new catch phrase for Back To Nature."

"You don't like it?" He paused, straightened.

Jackie felt the magnetic draw of his personality. Any man who could single-handedly run a major network at thirty-some-years-old possessed definite charisma.

She cleared her throat against the sudden thickness lodged there. "I like it. I just wanted to go on the record as saying I don't think 'follow your natural instincts' is a very good idea when it comes down to you and me."

6

How could being in complete and utter accord with a woman still cause such agony? Greg tried to think through the problem logically the next morning as he entered Studio A for his first full day on a production crew in years.

He and Jackie had agreed on everything last night—the vivid greens used in the new set, the addition of misters to make the jungle scene more steamy, and most of all, they were in staunch concurrence they would *not* follow their natural instincts.

All that agreement was making him irritable as hell considering the only thing he *really* wanted to do was rewind to last weekend before he'd ever crossed professional paths with Jackie.

Of course, it didn't help that she was already on the set this morning, lounging from a tree branch in their fake jungle backdrop. Clad in the ragged tan suede bikini, one long leg dangling from the banyan branches, Jackie had his mouth watering before 9:00 a.m. How the hell would he survive an eight-hour day?

Greg started toward that lone long leg, drawn toward Jackie like magnetic north. Halfway there, his administrative assistant stepped in his path, waving a folder full of pink message notes.

"Morning, Chip," Greg grumbled, his eyes never leaving Jackie.

"Thought you might want to review yesterday's calls between takes this morning." Chip followed Greg's gaze to the prehistoric, tree-dwelling goddess. "Also, your brother went to get some breakfast, but he was here earlier and he said he needs to talk to you."

Greg couldn't concentrate on Mike's crisis with Chip clearly ogling Jackie. Where the hell was a tablecloth when a man needed one? Greg wanted to shield every inch of her from his assistant's avid stare.

"Thanks, Chip, but you'd better get back upstairs so you can cover for me this morning. With any luck, we'll finish this shoot in the next couple of days and things will get back to normal."

Chip nodded, but it took him a damn long time to tear his gaze away from Jackie. The kid looked like a cartoon character with frigging big red hearts in his eyes.

Unable to stop himself, Greg snapped his fingers in front of the kid's face.

Chip startled, the cartoon hearts fading away as he turned back into his capable self. "You bet. The network execs called too, sir, and they wanted to let you know they're moving up their quarterly meeting. They're flying out here the end of next week."

Greg could practically feel the cartoon hearts vanishing from his own eyes as reality cold-cocked him. "Please tell me you made that last part up."

His assistant clutched his chest as if mortally offended. "I take the best messages in the building, sir.

That's why they assigned me to the penthouse." He straightened his suspenders and backed toward the door. "In fact, I'm heading back upstairs right now to make sure I don't miss anything else. You want me to call the network and tell them next week won't work for you?"

And have them wondering what was going on at WBCI that the general manager couldn't take a few hours to meet with them? "Definitely not." He waved the file folder full of pink papers in salutation and headed toward the set. "Thanks for the messages, Chip. You're doing a great job."

As his assistant beamed his way out the studio door, Greg had to admit *he* was the only one who was falling down on the job lately. He'd hired a less than stellar job candidate for the voice-over talent because he'd been too stubborn to work with Jackie. Then he'd agreed to a week's stint as a producer when he was supposed to be running his station. Sure he'd done it partly because he didn't want to lose a high-profile account, but—if he was honest with himself—he'd probably also done it because he missed the hands-on side of production after years in a purely managerial position.

What a great time for the network execs to come for a visit.

A sultry voice called down from the tree above him. "You look a bit cantankerous for a man walking through jungle paradise. Don't you like the way the set came together?"

Greg closed his eyes for a two-count, willing away his automatic response to her perfect contralto. By the time he looked up, her leg no longer dangled from the branches but carried her bikini-clad body down the tree with a seductive shimmy.

She landed with an elegant thud beside him, her dancer's grace obvious whether she wore kitty ears or suede beach attire. Flipping her cinnamon curls over one bare shoulder, she stared up at the pseudo-jungle in front of them.

"It looks pretty real to me," she continued, oblivious to the true source of his irritability as she hopped from one restless foot to another. No doubt Jackie wasn't the kind of woman who would be content to sit idle in a tree—or in a slow-moving production—for long. "I don't think we could get much more authentic without taking the whole production on location. Do you?"

He blinked past his body's response to the expanse of bare skin exposed by her skimpy outfit and focused on her words.

"Location? As in a ten-day nightmare of waiting for the sun and clouds to cooperate so we can capture the right lighting? I don't think so." No way would he sacrifice his general manager duties for all that time just to please the whim of a client. Moreover, no way would he subject himself to the pleasurable torment of being with Jackie for that long. "The set looks great."

She reached to trace the stringy bark of a spurious vine hanging from the tree. Tugging on it, she seemed to test its strength to bear her weight, then wrapped one long leg around the vine and swung past him, hair flying behind her. "I think so too."

Greg's mouth went dry at the strands of cinnamon

silk brushed his shoulder. Wasn't it just peachy being in accord?

"I'm going to go take a look at it through the camera lens and see what kind of image we're getting." Yes indeed. Much safer to watch Jackie arching her back as she soared through the air via a camera lens.

Or so he hoped.

Soon, Greg immersed himself in the old routine of adjusting tripods and choosing the right films for still shots in addition to live action. He'd missed the creative immersion inherent to production work, a pleasure he'd quickly tossed aside in his pursuit to scale greater professional heights.

Absorbed in fine-tuning the lighting bouncing off Jackie's pale skin, Greg didn't notice his brother until a burly shadow messed up his wattage levels.

"You call this work?" Mike asked, waving a bag of fast food under Greg's nose. "How much of a challenge can it be to light a gorgeous woman's body? Doesn't she pretty much look phenomenal no matter what you do?"

Greg snatched the sausage- and egg-scented paper sack and tossed it on a rolling cart next to his phone and his mountain of unreturned messages. He did not want to discuss Jackie Brady's merits with his brother.

And damn it, he didn't *ever* want to remember his brother had seen her nearly naked too.

"Every job presents a unique challenge. Right now I'm trying to find a happy medium with the light so there's enough to highlight her outfit but not enough to overexpose her skin." As Greg stared down into his camera lens to check the effect of his latest attempt, Jackie waved a friendly hello to Mike.

And his big, burly, doofus brother waved back.

Greg ground his teeth together and restrained himself from elbowing him. In a low voice, he reminded him, "No flirting with the talent."

Especially not Jackie.

Whom Mike had seen half-naked.

"She knows how to send sparks flying, doesn't she?" Mike whispered back, his gaze as captivated by the suede bikini as Chip had been.

Damn it, he didn't even appreciate the half of how phenomenal she was if all he could see was the damn skimpy outfit.

"What the hell does that mean?" Greg stepped back from the camera, dragging his brother along with him. "How dare you notice sparks from any woman but Hannah. I thought you were going to try to win her back?"

Mike shook his head. His shoulders slumped. "She won't even let me see her. I tried to talk to her yesterday but she wouldn't even open the door. Said she's working on self-transformation." He spread his arms wide, the Italian in him talking with his hands. "As if I'd want her any different than just the way she is."

Greg struggled to make sense of the situation. "I thought she dumped you because of your wandering eye?"

"Damn it, Greg, I knew you were only half-listening to me yesterday. Yes, she thinks I look at other women too much, even though you and I both know I'd never think about cheating on her." Mike shook his head, the picture of despair. "And according to her she only worries about that because she's insecure. She's got it in her head that she needs to be sure there are real sparks flying in both directions." Mike looked back toward Jackie, who was using the downtime on the set to perfect her vine swinging.

If Greg didn't get back to work soon, she'd be taking out his tripods.

Couldn't the woman sit still for two seconds?

"She wants sparks flying," Greg repeated, trying to hang on to the story this time. "Understandable."

Mike rolled his eyes. "Yeah, but instead of asking me about turning up the heat a bit, guess who Hannah asked for help in the sparks department?"

Greg hadn't a clue.

Until Mike angled his head toward the restless songbird swinging from the ceiling.

"Jackie's helping Hannah..." Greg couldn't seem to force the words past his lips.

"...figure out how to light a man's fire," Mike finished for him. "How's that for a lethal combo? The cat stripper turned jungle woman takes naive schoolteacher under her wing."

"She's not a stripper," Greg replied on autopilot.

"Yeah, yeah, exotic dancer. Whatever."

Greg gritted his teeth, his thoughts reeling with the notion of Jackie Brady giving lessons in seduction.

Despite her protests that she wanted to keep things professional between them, Jackie had decided to teach her feminine wiles for other women to unleash on unsuspecting De Costa men.

And damn it, for all Greg knew, she was plotting his seduction right now too. Maybe that was all part of her ploy when she wrapped her bare leg around that vine like a lover.

She had probably already gone to work on him!

Greg took deep breaths, searching for a modicum of professional distance before he confronted Jackie about this.

One thing was certain.

They sure as hell weren't in accord any longer.

JACKIE DIDN'T KNOW IF SHE could stand working in film for another minute.

How did actors and actresses bear this sort of vast wasteland of downtime while production people wreaked their magic? Jackie usually performed in sound studios where you didn't need to worry about appearances.

And even then, singing had always been only half of her dream. Even more than she wanted to sing, she wanted to compose.

Yet instead of getting closer to her dream, Jackie feared she'd moved further away by taking the Back To Nature commercial. Sure she would have a speaking spot with national exposure, but she was sacrificing days of great composing time to swing idly from the trees.

Would this commercial clip increase her marketability enough as a singer to warrant the loss of writing time?

She didn't have long to ponder the matter, however, as the too-sexy-for-his-own-good general manager currently strode toward her, a stern set to his jaw.

She stuffed her dreams to the back of her mind, a hiding place they were long accustomed to after growing up in a world where convention was king. Later, she would debate the wisdom of her career path and figure out how to keep herself on track.

Right now, she had a cranky GM to please.

"Are we ready to start shooting?" she asked, hoping she sounded enthusiastic as opposed to bored out of her mind. She jumped off the makeshift vine to stand face-to-face with the man who'd starred in some very explicit dreams the night before.

Greg, however, didn't look very pleased.

"No. We are not ready to start shooting." He barely articulated the words around his clenched teeth. "In fact, I don't know if we're ever going to be ready to start shooting given that you've gone back on your word to keep things strictly professional between us."

Unspoken accusations clearly glared from his dark-brown eyes.

Over his shoulder, she noticed his brother fade into the background, as did the lone stylist on the set. Apparently the rest of the people who knew Greg De Costa knew when to stay out of his way.

Lucky for her, Jackie had never backed down from a scene.

She straightened, meeting his gaze with a level look

of her own. "I think you'd better watch how you frame this discussion, Greg, because I can see you're going to end up doing a lot of apologizing here. Unless, of course, you call wearing the costume Shamus Fletcher chose for me as me being unprofessional." She shook the fringe of her suede bikini with an obvious wiggle. "I can see where this is borderline risqué, but believe me, I wasn't consulted on wardrobe for this shoot."

For a moment, some of the anger in Greg's eyes changed to something far more interesting and... heated.

Jackie wondered if he'd forget all about the anger if she tugged him closer by those suspenders of his and kissed him with everything she had.

She'd barely had time to indulge the fantasy when Greg frowned all the harder.

"*That's* exactly the kind of thing I'm talking about."

"Okay, pardon me if I haven't had my coffee yet and my brain isn't necessarily clicking along at full speed. *What* exactly are you talking about?" She hopped from foot to foot to keep warm in the drafty studio.

"The whole—" he pointed an accusing finger at her breasts "—shimmy thing you just did. Don't try to tell me that's not part of your carefully crafted seduction scheme."

How could he think such a thing? "Trust me, Greg, if I was scheming to seduce you, we'd be too busy ripping our clothes off right now to debate the issue."

He opened his mouth to speak, but no sound issued forth. Judging by the intense heat of his eyes, Jackie had the feeling Greg was too busy envisioning that very scenario.

When he finally spoke, his words carried the husky rasp of a man who'd run a marathon. "But you can't deny you're giving lessons in seduction to Hannah Williams. Can you?"

So that's what this was about. Jackie relaxed just a little. He certainly had no right to hold that against her.

"So what if I am?" She backed up a step to maneuver the vine in between them. Holding it with both hands, she allowed the prop to hang down in front of her like a shield. "You and I agreed to keep things professional between us. I don't see how that prohibits me from befriending your future sister-in-law."

Greg peered around the studio before answering, as if to be certain no one could overhear them. "Befriending is one thing. Giving her lessons in seduction is another. I can't think about you doing *that* and still make a good commercial, Jackie. It's like giving my imagination free reign to fantasize nonstop."

"And that's my fault?" She could hardly be responsible for his fantasies. "I don't think so. Why don't we get back to shooting now and put this commercial to bed so we can go about our lives, okay?"

Greg's dark eyes turned almost black. He ran his hand down the length of his silk tie and nodded slowly. "You want to put this to bed, do you?"

Okay, maybe it hadn't been the greatest choice of wording given the charged atmosphere.

"Yes."

"And you're going to continue to teach seduction as if it were a damn art form?"

She licked lips gone dry and clutched the vine a little more tightly. But she wouldn't back down, damn it. "As long as Hannah wants me to, then, yes, I will."

"Then as far as I'm concerned, all bets are off between us."

"Meaning?" she asked even though she wasn't all that sure she wanted to know.

"Meaning if you're hell-bent on parading this kind of continual provocation right under my nose, then I'm not going to force myself to ignore it any longer." His voice projected a little more with every word until anyone hanging about the fringes of the set would be able to hear them.

Jackie had never minded causing a commotion before, but she wasn't so sure how she felt about publicizing their brief romantic interlude.

"Umm...okay." She forced a smile to keep things light—probably a doomed proposition. "Why don't we get back to shooting now and that way we can stick to schedule?"

"Fine by me." He smiled for the first time since he'd heard her demo tape. "But first, are we still on for this weekend?"

Her heart hammered away at her chest.

She blinked. He couldn't mean what she thought he meant, because they had definitely cancelled their date. "I don't think the shooting schedule says anything about working on the weekends, but if we need to—"

He leaned close enough to heat the two inches of air between them, close enough to make her very aware of her lack of clothes.

His eyes locked on hers. "I'm not talking about working. I'm talking about our *date*."

The word lingered in the air, teasing Jackie with possibility.

"We decided that was not a good idea." Too bad her voice had dipped into a sultry range she scarcely recognized and was broadcasting a message all its own.

She tore her gaze away from his, but all she could focus on was his shoulders encased in the blue broadcloth of his dress shirt.

And his suspenders.

"I think it's a very good idea," he countered, tipping her chin up with one hand. "After all, won't you need someone to practice those seduction techniques on? How could I, in good conscience, allow you to teach it to Hannah all wrong?"

A smile hitched the corners of her lips. Greg was far too potent for a mere mortal woman to resist. Sure, he possessed some of the same rigid attitudes that had driven her crazy growing up in her parents' home. And he was obviously on a fast track career-wise that Jackie would never want for herself.

But he had a charismatic energy that drew her like the tide to the moon. As long as she didn't delude herself that this interlude was forever, perhaps she could indulge in all that masculine charm and heat for just a little while.

"Okay. But just remember who's in charge once Saturday rolls around."

"Meaning?"

"Meaning you might be lord of the network and the producer-director of this television commercial, but when it comes to seduction, Greg, I direct all the action."

She leaned close enough to tease his chest with the fringe of her suede costume, close enough to whisper in his ear.

"And it's up to you to follow my lead wherever I want to go."

7

"YOU TOLD HIM TO FOLLOW *your* lead?" Hannah hugged her knees closer to her chest as they sat on Jackie's living room floor Saturday afternoon. She sounded half scandalized and half enthralled. "Are we talking about the same Greg De Costa here—Mr. All-Business?"

Jackie smiled as she cut out another pink paper bunny ear for Hannah's kindergarten class and recalled her close encounter with Greg in the studio a few days ago. He hadn't seemed all business when he'd been exchanging gulps of preheated oxygen with her on the Back To Nature set.

"I have the feeling I bring out a different side of Greg," she admitted. "And it's not a side he necessarily likes in himself. But I find all that restrained charm incredibly sexy."

In fact, all week she'd found everything about Greg incredibly sexy. So much so that she couldn't help but wonder if he was the man to break her lifelong dry spell.

Then again, she thought as she cut around a tight curve in the bunny ear, maybe she was just making any excuse to be with Greg. Even if it was just for a night.

Or a weekend. Maybe a *long* weekend.

Snip—she accidentally amputated poor Fluffy's ear.

"I could never tell Mike I wanted to take the lead." Hannah jammed her scissors into another white paper plate that would serve as the hat part of the bunny ears. She cut the inside of the plate out so her students could wear them around their heads.

Jackie slapped her pathetic attempt at a pink inner rabbit ear onto the towering pile of construction paper and then pried herself off the floor, carefully avoiding the plastic sacks full of cotton balls. "Are you kidding? Not only will you *tell* him you're taking the lead, you're going to have your way with that man until all he sees is you."

Hannah snorted. "Look at me." She gestured toward her long stretchy skirt and baggy pink T-shirt. "I've got schoolteacher written all over me. I don't think Mike's suddenly going to start drooling no matter how many inches I hike up this hem. He's certainly had plenty of opportunities to demonstrate his physical affection, if you know what I mean."

The timer on the stove started beeping, calling Jackie into the kitchen.

"Forget naked thighs. It's all about attitude." Or so Jackie hoped. She'd lose her nerve about the whole "follow my lead" thing if she thought thighs counted.

She pulled their lunch—a cookie sheet full of potato skins, heavy on the chives—out of the oven and searched her fridge for sour cream. "Maybe Mike's just too shy to put the moves on you before the wedding. Or too old-fashioned."

Hannah held up her paper plate creation. "Or

maybe I just need to wear rabbit ears and a little cotton tail. The guys really seemed to go for your cat suit. Who's to say bunnies aren't sexy?"

Jackie plunked their feast on the coffee table, complete with pink lemonade. "It worked for Hugh Hefner's crew because their rabbit getups were more satin and fur than construction paper I think, Hannah."

"Okay, so we've determined I'm getting a major attitude adjustment so I can turn Mike's head for a change." Hannah munched her potato while Jackie opened the doors to her balcony so the spring air and the sounds of the quiet Boston street could drift through the apartment.

"Right." Jackie slid back to the floor and took up her potato skin for some major snacking.

"But what's *your* plan of attack with Greg tonight?"

Butterflies flapped their way through Jackie's stomach, suddenly robbing her of her appetite. She dropped a half-eaten skin back onto her plate.

"I don't know. The sparks-flying stage is about the extent of my knowledge base." She didn't want to think about her date tonight. All week her interaction with Greg had been fraught with sizzle and loaded with steam. What if she couldn't deliver on all the heat she promised?

Furthermore, they'd developed a solid working rapport beyond all the seductive glances. What if tonight's romantic engagement somehow messed that up? Jackie's fledgling career couldn't afford any slips.

In order to hide her moment of panic, she shifted the conversation back to Hannah and Mike. "I want to know when you're going to affect this attitude adjustment, Ms. Williams. If you don't see Mike, you'll never have the chance to seduce him."

Hannah flashed her a wicked grin. "I'm going to see him. Tonight."

"You go, girl!" Jackie squealed over her new friend's tentative agreement to see her jilted fiancé again. "Good for you to face Mike on your own terms. Where are you going to get together?"

"I told him to meet me in Harvard Square." She gasped, her eyes widening. "Why don't you meet Greg there, too? We can impart some girl-power to one another and at least get past the initial awkward greeting stage."

"I wouldn't want to intrude—"

"You wouldn't be. In fact, I really need you there. You have to come for moral support."

Hope simmered through Jackie. If she and Greg could bump into Hannah and Mike, it would take some of the sensual pressure off the evening. No matter how much Jackie had thought about Greg this week, she was still a little nervous about seeing one another outside the studio.

And she was even more nervous about trying to entice him into an intimate scenario that put her in the driver's seat. She might talk a good game, but she had zero experience in the sex department. Her relationships with struggling artists had always exploded in her face before developing much heat.

"Just come to the square around seven and we'll all

find each other." Hannah spooned more sour cream on her plate as she sat cross-legged on the floor, her stretchy cotton skirt tucked around her feet. "Last spring Mike took me to the Public Garden for a swan boat ride, but this year, we're going to do something more wild to celebrate the rites of spring. I'm going to show him the *other* side of the kindergarten teacher— the untamed woman within."

"Are you really serious about calling off the wedding, Hannah?" Jackie had since learned their date was only two weeks away. Mike had his bachelor party early because Greg's work schedule was so hectic.

Jackie couldn't envision marriage in her foreseeable future given all that she wanted to achieve in her career. And okay, it probably also hurt her chances that the only way she could secure a date these days was via impromptu striptease.

But she couldn't imagine throwing love away with both hands like Hannah seemed to be doing.

"I'm very serious. I don't want to get married simply for love." Hannah tapped one squared, unpolished fingernail against her tiled drink coaster—a mosaic stone depiction of a man and woman kissing. "I want passion. And I want to know that Mike can look at other women all he wants, but that at the end of the day, he'll still only want *me*."

"A perfectly reasonable wish." Jackie toyed with her own drink coaster—a small reproduction of the famous WWII photo of a sailor laying a major smooch on girl in a cute dress. Jackie had purchased the set on

Newbury Street at an art fair but had never completely appreciated the lush ardent themes painted on each one until just now.

Did she harbor as much romance in her soul as Hannah seemed to?

A scary thought considering Jackie had already determined any encounter with Greg would be strictly to follow up on their major attraction while avoiding romantic entanglements. Jackie had attempted a total of two relationships since college, both of which had been big letdowns. And both of those guys had been bona fide artists—men with as much passion about their work as Jackie had about hers.

If she couldn't make things work with a stand-up comic or a caricaturist, how on earth could she ever succeed with a fast track, corporate guy who placed more emphasis on the politics of networking than creating great art?

A relationship would only hurt them both.

Which was all the more reason Jackie needed to work up enough courage to stick with Plan A to keep things between them simple and—a tingle of anticipation jumped through her veins—sensual.

She and Greg would have a fling. If only she could unearth a little of her usual daring, she wanted very much to kiss her virginity goodbye tonight. As long as she remained in control of what happened between them, she'd be fine.

With any luck—and a lot of nerve—maybe by tomorrow she'd be ready to embrace passion for her art and she could walk away from the messy complications of romance.

For once, Jackie had come up with a perfect plan.

GREG DIDN'T KNOW WHOSE idea it was to get together with his brother and his brother's estranged fiancée on the night he was supposed to finally get Jackie alone, but he sure as hell didn't like it.

Yet here he sat in a basement pub at a booth near the Irish fiddler while he watched Jackie, Hannah and his brother walking toward him across the planked floor.

Obviously, Mike was too concerned about making things right with Hannah to cry foul on the double date setup. But Mike didn't look all that happy with the arrangement either.

Jackie, on the other hand, seemed right in her element.

Greg wondered if the performer in her might feel more comfortable in a group than one-on-one. An intriguing contradiction after all her provocative talk and seductive promises.

She slid into the booth alongside him, her tiny white tank top tucked into drawstring khakis while her shoulders swam in a loose denim jacket. "Look who I found."

Her voice—which Greg had grown to know intimately over the past week in the studio—had a breathless note.

Anticipation? Or nervousness he hadn't expected to find in a woman who seemed at home with commotion?

Curious, Greg held her gaze, silently questioning. "A happy coincidence." He nodded a greeting to his brother and then turned his attention to Hannah. "Nice to see you."

Unlike Jackie, there wasn't a hint of anything remotely close to nervous energy surrounding Hannah. Greg had never seen her look more relaxed and in control. A quiet sense of purpose emanated from her intelligent blue eyes, a force of personality that even her long floral skirt and sweater set didn't begin to soften.

Clearly, she was a woman on a mission.

"Likewise." She sat across from Jackie and smiled. "I hear your current production is destined for national release."

Mike leaned into the conversation, edging one elbow onto the table. "You ought to see Jackie dressed up as Jane. She swings out of this tree on a vine and—"

Greg could see precisely when Mike jammed his size twelve foot into his mouth. Had to hurt.

If a guy got dumped for noticing other women, it probably wasn't the greatest idea to rave about a half-dressed jungle goddess.

Although, heaven knew, Greg had entertained enough fantasies about playing Tarzan to her Jane that he had a pretty good idea how distracting a jungle goddess could be.

Empathizing, he jumped in to save his brother's bacon. "It's a feat of set engineering Jackie came up with," Greg continued. "She couldn't just hang out in the tree. She had to have the vine to swing on too. The client is totally blown away by her."

Understatement of the year. Shamus was practically

in love with her if the adoring looks he sent her way were any indication.

Greg could only hope those looks were the result of Shamus seeing dollar signs in Jackie's memorable voice and energetic delivery rather than some sort of May-December romantic delusion taken to the extreme.

A waitress dropped four menus on the table as she skirted past them with a tray packed full of beer bottles lined up like bowling pins for a strike. "I'll be with you folks in a minute," she called over her shoulder.

Hannah pushed the menus toward Greg. "Actually, we can't stay." She picked up her purse and slid out from under the table, casting a conspiratorial wink toward Jackie. "I think I'm going to be brave enough to face tonight on my own after all. Besides, Mike and I have a lot of...talking to do."

Go, Hannah.

Greg couldn't help but smile at his brother's bewildered expression. Mike had a lot to learn about women and Greg, for one, was damn well pleased Hannah had decided he was worth the time to teach.

Okay, and maybe part of him was just thrilled he could be alone with Jackie now.

"Are you sure?" Jackie's brow furrowed as she watched the couple stand.

"Definitely." Hannah nodded. "It's probably time we *both* put those lessons into practice."

With a few parting salutations, they disappeared into the crush of Saturday night Boston revelers.

Leaving Jackie and Greg very close together in a semiprivate booth.

Excellent.

Now he only needed to ensure Jackie wanted something to happen between them tonight as much as he did.

He pushed away the menus resting between them and turned toward her in his seat.

She looked gorgeous. There was a simple beauty about her, a down-to-earth appeal that didn't require a lot of decoration. She'd probably been wearing the same jean jacket since high school and her khakis looked like they'd seen more than a few weekends at the Cape. Greg suspected that—underneath her center-of-attention personality—the woman was as tried and true as her wardrobe.

"You're the one in charge tonight, Jackie," he reminded her. "Why don't you make the call what happens next."

They could walk the maze of Boston's downtown streets and watch the stars. He could order her a plate of the pub's famous oysters and then test their powers as an aphrodisiac. Or they could discuss Greg's recurring Tarzan thoughts....

His erotic imaginings were interrupted when he noted her expression. Was it his imagination or did a fleeting look of panic cross her face?

"Why don't we go to the studio?" she blurted.

"Hmm?" Surely he'd misunderstood.

"We haven't really done much with the soundtrack for the commercial and I thought we could try out some jingles." She bit her lip for a moment, then plowed ahead. "I've had a couple of tunes running through my head that might be—"

"Let me get this straight. You want to work tonight?" Greg shook his head to clear it of any cobwebs. He hadn't had a single beer, though God knows a drink was sounding good right about now.

"You're showing the commercial to the client on Monday, right?" With restless fingers, Jackie spun the heavy man's watch she wore around and around her wrist.

He nodded. "I hope you can be there to rake in the kudos on a job well done. I'm meeting Shamus and his board at ten o'clock."

She stopped spinning the watch. "Then we ought to head to the studio. You wouldn't want to miss an opportunity to make the commercial even better, would you?"

If it meant he'd get to taste Jackie's dessert wine kisses again, hell yes, he'd gladly miss out on the opportunity.

But maybe she was just nervous. For that matter, maybe she'd changed her mind. Whatever the case may be, Greg would see the evening through and hope for the best.

He had the feeling he probably looked as bewildered as his brother had a few minutes ago...when Greg had so smugly thought *Mike* had a lot to learn about women.

Seemed like he didn't have a clue either.

"I'll go on one condition," he finally agreed.

Her smile beamed with more wattage than professional studio lighting. "Name it."

"You do all your recording in the Jane getup."

She rolled her eyes as she slid out of the booth. "You stand about as much chance of seeing me strut around in that bikini as I do of seeing you in a loincloth. No deal." She tugged her keys out of her jacket pocket and dangled them in the air. "Don't forget who's in the driver's seat tonight."

FAT CHANCE GREG WOULD forget who was in the driver's seat.

Jackie had nearly killed them on the way over to the studio in her age-old white convertible Bug. But then, she'd been too nervous about tonight to concentrate on the windy back road that led to WBCI.

She'd had a small panic attack in the booth at the pub when Greg has asked her what she'd like to do tonight. How did a woman go about demanding a sexual interlude? Jackie's mother may have failed to turn her into a proper lady on several counts, but Jackie had retained enough sense of refinement to know that wasn't the type of thing she could come right out and request.

So she'd blurted the first thing that entered her edgy thoughts. Let's sing.

God, he must think she was a total moron.

Even now, as Greg escorted them into the quiet building, tense energy hummed through her. Some of that nervous tension was purely sexual. But a little was work-related. As a result of tonight's bumbling, she had somehow talked him into letting her try recording a jingle.

Maybe he'd only agreed at first to be nice, but by the time Jackie was through dazzling him right out of his socks, he'd want to use the catchy song for its own merit.

A few staffers manned the television station at night, but Studio A was completely dark when they arrived. The jungle set stood in shadow in the middle of the floor, but that wasn't what caught Jackie's eye.

A small sound studio and editing room connected to the area where filming took place. As she watched, Greg flipped a switch on the panel near the door, turning on only the light in the glass-enclosed soundbooth.

During their days of shooting, only Greg had ever entered that off-limits technology center.

Tonight, Jackie would have her turn.

She channeled her nerves into creativity—now ready and eager to put on a pair of headphones and start singing. After she'd captured her tune on tape, maybe she'd have the confidence to follow up on her major attraction to Greg. Something about singing gave her a mental high, a total self-assurance she couldn't get anywhere else.

Halfway to the sound mecca, Greg's voice called after her. "You're really jazzed about recording this, aren't you?"

Caught. Jackie slowed herself, forced herself to wait for him. He was really being so accommodating about her unorthodox request. Her genius composer parents had never had nearly as much patience for her off-the-wall methods of working.

"It's like that rush of energy you get when you've studied for a test." She stood behind him as he used his master key to unlock the door. She couldn't help but notice the broad expanse of his back in his gray shirt, the square set of his shoulders underneath wine colored suspenders. She wondered if he'd wear those suspenders to a Red Sox game or if he owned a T-shirt. "You just want to get in there and get it over with."

"Then by all means, be my guest." He held the door open for her as he stood half in the door frame.

Jackie edged past, careful not to brush against any part of him yet electrically aware of how close their bodies came to touching. A hint of his musky aftershave beckoned her closer.

So did his dark, watchful gaze.

Her heart kicked up the pace, alerting her to the distraction Greg presented. She couldn't afford to miss out on her opportunity to impress him.

She breathed a sigh of relief as she made it by him, but her sense of reprieve didn't last for long. The sound room was roughly the size of a linen closet.

Greg seemed to surround her as he pulled out a chair for her with one hand and reached down under the desk for a pair of headphones with his other. His tie fell against her spine, a whisper of silk her heightened nerves could feel straight through her denim jacket.

A shiver of pure sensual hunger trembled through her and it didn't have a damn thing to do with the headphones he handed her or with the opportunity to sing her jingle.

This shiver was all about Greg De Costa.

"Cold?" he asked her as she took a seat inside the narrow space.

She nodded to cover her obvious reaction, not trusting her voice in the wake of a mouth gone dry.

His smile assured her he saw straight through her. "It'll warm up in here in no time."

She didn't doubt that for a minute. The tiny space of the recording studio immersed her in the scent, sound and sight of Greg.

Jamming her headphones over her ears, Jackie attempted to drag her thoughts away from Greg's male appeal and refocus on the jingle she'd convinced herself she needed to record tonight.

"Testing, testing." The words came through her earpiece loud and clear as Greg flipped the switch to connect their audio and begin the current commercial soundtrack.

His voice had a smooth delivery and depth of pitch she'd noticed but never really thought about before.

"Did you come up through the ranks in radio?" she asked, speaking into the microphone he adjusted in front of her.

"I went from the piano bar to the Morning Zoo on a low-budget FM station." He winked at her as he loaded a new roll of tape into a recording slot. "You might have woken up to my voice while you were a teenager."

Something vaguely naughty about that image made

her smile. "My parents were introducing me to Chopin then, so I usually awoke to piano movements. I felt lucky to get away with setting the dial to National Public Radio."

At his puzzled expression, Jackie realized she'd never told him about her family.

"My mother and father are celebrated composers. They still travel a lot to play with orchestras around the country."

Greg snapped his fingers in recognition. "Your dad is Niall Brady?"

Of course he would be impressed. Who wasn't impressed?

Jackie truly was proud of her parents, they were just a hard act to follow. Especially as she sat here with headphones on ready to belt out a tune for Greg for the first time since her kitty costume fell off.

"That's my dad. My mom is—"

"Deirdre Breslin Brady. Our news team did a feature piece on them a couple of years ago when I was still in production. Your dad wanted to hear all about my years playing piano in the bar."

"Yes, well, he's not so forgiving of those kinds of musical choices within his own family." No sooner had she spoken the words than she realized how ungrateful she sounded. "Not that there's anything wrong with your musical choices, of course—" She sighed. "Is my family baggage showing through here a bit?"

Greg laughed. "You've certainly clarified why you own a pair of cymbals. You ready to get to work?"

Just like that, he'd put an end to an awkward moment.

While Greg waited, his tape loaded and ready to go, Jackie couldn't help but think he really was a great guy.

So what if he had sold out on his creative skill by leaving production work for his corporate penthouse? He sure knew how to put a person at ease.

Now more than ever, she knew he was the perfect man to end her reign as a twenty-four-year-old virgin.

Tonight.

8

ANTICIPATION CHURNING through her, Jackie nodded. She could already begin to appreciate how much depth of passion an intimate encounter would bring to her music. Just thinking about being with Greg made her want to sing.

She pulled a beat-up harmonica out of her pocket, unapologetic for her own creative oddities. That harmonica had been the first musical instrument she'd bought for herself—something simple, accessible, that still managed to be beautiful.

Finding her middle C on the mouthpiece, Jackie hummed out the note, allowing it to vibrate all the way to the roots of her hair. With the pure sound still echoing through the room, she closed her eyes and set aside the instrument now that she was attuned to her key.

She sang her upbeat jingle into the microphone, focused solely on giving a solid performance. Technically, she knew they could retake the tune several times until she nailed it just right, but Jackie wasn't half as concerned about the recording as she was about Greg's impression of her work.

The suggestive lyrics for the Back To Nature tune came to her while she'd been getting ready for their date tonight—a spin-off on Greg's "follow your natural instincts" theme.

Surprise, surprise, she'd come up with something racy in the process of daydreaming about Greg.

But the song wasn't just sexy. Jackie sang it with a teasing note, a hint of laughter that lightened the message.

At least that was the intent.

"...So in any situation, just follow your natural inclination." She reached down deep for the final notes of her song, taking the music up a level for a high-octane finish. "And get Back To Nature with me!"

As she finished humming the final bars of the background music that had yet to be recorded for the jingle, Jackie looked to Greg for his reaction.

She'd hoped to see a smile of approval perhaps.

What she found instead was a heated look that could have thrust even the most reserved woman into major meltdown mode.

As Jackie's temporary producer, Greg knew he should have broken out in applause or at least given her a two thumbs-up in the wake of her clever, marketable tune.

Too bad he couldn't move an inch without fearing he'd touch her. Taste her. Take her down to the floor of the tiny sound studio and undress her with his hands as thoroughly as he had stripped her in his mind.

He was in the grip of some sort of lust paralysis, damn it, and he barely trusted himself to breathe.

With new appreciation, he realized how half the

men in the U.S. felt after Marilyn Monroe sang her breathy Happy Birthday to J.F.K.

"Greg?" Jackie's voice whispered through the far-too-small studio and feathered along his senses.

She sat mere inches away from him, their leather swivel armchairs almost touching. Her khaki-covered knee grazed his thigh.

"Hmm?" Obviously, he'd been robbed of his speech capacity as well.

"The lyrics are too overt, aren't they? Or maybe you didn't like the rhythm?" Worry furrowed her brow, her green eyes losing some of the fierce glitter they seemed to adopt when she sang.

No! His brain shouted a protest to her concerns, but suppressed lust had his body ignoring all incoming messages except one.

And damn it, he was going to listen to that message, if only to erase the oncoming cloud of disappointment in her eyes.

He reached for her, skimming one hand up her shoulder, the other to tip her mouth toward his. He stared down at her long enough to see the glittery shine return to her green gaze, the dark pupils dilating with the same desire he felt in every vein.

Her lips sighed hungry agreement as his mouth met hers. The dessert wine taste of her went straight to his head, fueling the fantasies he'd been having about this woman all week long.

Jackie in Nike high-tops and a tail.

Jackie swinging from a tree in a suede bikini, a vine snaking around one thigh.

And his personal favorite, Jackie in flame-red panties with bare breasts, her taut pink nipples peaked and ready for his touch.

He wanted to pull her into his lap, run his hands over every last inch of her generously curved body.

As he gripped her hips, however, she pushed lightly at his shoulders.

"Wait." Her breath came in little huffs, her cheeks flushed.

Greg released his hold on her, but couldn't back away quite yet. "Waiting" for a woman as red-hot as Jackie Brady might prove a bigger challenge than coming up with innovative programming during sweeps week.

"What is it?" His words rasped out in the close, sultry air of the small space.

She met his gaze, her own breathing satisfyingly ragged. "I don't want you to kiss me out of pity or anything. If you thought the song was that bad, I deserve to know."

Huh? The lust paralysis was a damn difficult affliction to shake. A full three-count must have passed while Greg made sense of what she was saying.

At which point the weight of her anxious words fell on him like an anvil on Saturday morning cartoons.

"Hell, no." He edged himself away from her, his need to set her straight smashing through the fog of runaway longing. "Your song is fantastic. In fact, it's so damn good I guess I figured you knew it."

How could a woman with her level of talent not know she was incredible?

"Really?" She fiddled with the harmonica that still rested in her hands, flipping it back and forth across her palm. "You don't think the suggestive parts are too...well, suggestive?"

He had to laugh at that one despite the insistent hunger for her, the overwhelming need to get her wrapped back up in a kiss and in his arms. "I don't think most male listeners would jump you after hearing it the way I just did, if that's what you mean. It was the line about listening to your body's natural urges that did me in."

She shoved the harmonica back in the pocket of her faded denim jacket and smiled. "I was sort of proud of that part. Do you think we can use it in the commercial?"

Greg forced his mind to think work instead of personal wishes. "Shamus will insist on it the minute he hears it, Jackie. And even if he didn't, I would talk him into it. That jingle adds the layer of memorable-ness we've been looking for. This tune will wake people up in the middle of the night while it plays over and over in their heads. It couldn't be more dead-on perfect for this campaign."

She squealed like a starlet winning her first Oscar. "I wrote a jingle! A commercially viable, people-will-hear-it-on-their-TV advertising song." She flung her arms wide and wrapped Greg in an enthusiastic hug that was probably all about triumph and professional joy for her.

Was he a total cad to experience intense sexual yearning at the brief brush of her breasts?

Of course he was.

He should be offering to take her out for a celebration dinner or drink instead of plotting ways to take her home tonight. Where the hell was his legendary professionalism?

"I think we've got enough on tape for the client," he continued, taking deep breaths to counteract the rush of blood through his veins. "We'll let Shamus listen to it Monday and worry about recording the music afterward."

She nodded, the triumph in her eyes turning him on almost as much as her songbird voice.

But he respected her as a professional, damn it, and he owed her this moment of victory. He'd already robbed her of a great full-time voice-over job because he couldn't seem to balance the personal mixed with the professional.

Would he deny her this too?

Not a chance.

Before he could change his mind, he blurted the appropriate invitation. "So what do you say we celebrate back at the pub with the best bottle of champagne my expense account will afford us? We can toast the start of a stellar career."

A mischievous, oh-so-sexy smile crossed her lips.

"I've got a better idea." She reached toward him, then walked her finger slowly up one of his suspenders.

Did she not know she was toying with fire?

This nice-guy act was damn well going to kill him.

She leaned closer, her soft pink lips the sole focus of his attention.

Her words fanned his cheek. "Why don't we celebrate right here?"

JACKIE WAITED IN breathless anticipation, hoping the little bout of nervousness didn't show through.

If Greg continued to play the nice guy even after her proposition, or if he insisted on celebrating her success in style, she was going to be more than a little embarrassed.

He stretched across the master control area, and for a minute, Jackie thought he'd reached for his keys to the station. Instead, he laid his finger along one lever and lowered it down, plunging the small, glass-enclosed studio into darkness.

Her heart kicked into high speed, fast-forward.

In that moment of inky blackness, Greg must have found the control lever for the lighting over the Studio A set too, because a single lamp suddenly illuminated the jungle area where they'd shot their commercial. That lone spotlight some twenty-five yards away reflected dimly in their isolated glass booth.

Greg's silky radio voice floated through the shadows.

"Please say your idea of a celebration involves us getting much, much closer." His hands materialized on her hips, slid up to curve around her waist.

Electric sensation pulsed into her like a current, starting at his fingertips to zing through her every nerve ending, then gather in aching awareness somewhere deep between her thighs.

"My idea involves laying my body over yours like a

lyrical track over music." She rose out of her seat to settle herself in his armchair, straddling his body with a knee on either side. "Is that close enough for you?"

She'd never been so bold in all her life. And her mother had assured her on numerous occasions she was far too brazen.

Greg didn't look disappointed.

His low groan went right through her as he pulled her closer, sealing their bodies together from hip to chest. The heat and strength of him permeated her clothes, firing straight to her skin.

His mouth clamped down around hers, kissing her with a hunger as fierce and edgy as her own. She'd waited so long for this—this man and this night. She wanted everything he had to offer her and she wanted it immediately.

She wriggled her hips against him to be sure he knew as much.

The ragged moan from deep in his throat might have been a growl straight off the jungle soundtrack. "You're like one-hundred-proof whiskey, Jackie, and you're burning my insides the whole damn way down." His eyes glittered dark and predatory in the dim light. "I might need to build up a tolerance against you."

"That sounds far too cautious." She squeezed his waist with her thighs and undid his necktie. "I'm driving tonight so indulge all you want."

Her words had exactly the desired affect. He was stripping off her clothes before she'd gotten the whole sentence out.

"I want you naked." He pushed her denim jacket to the floor and reached for the hem of her tank top.

Never one to bother with a bra unless strictly necessary, Jackie delighted in Greg's string of appreciative oaths as he discovered that fact with his hands. As her shirt hit the industrial carpet, Greg's lips found her breasts, his tongue drawing sweet circles of homage around her nipples.

She arched back to increase the sensation, sighing at the gentle chafe of his jaw against her tender skin.

Her eyes drifted closed, but Jackie forced them open again, needing to drink in every possible sense from her night with Greg. Sultry heat surrounded them, foggy mist stole over the glass windowpanes of the booth.

Her gaze settled on Greg, his own eyes closed to taste her, his lashes a sooty crescent on his cheek.

Perhaps feeling the weight of her stare, he looked up at her, never slowing his thorough tasting. That electric current within sizzled double time, igniting a fire low in her belly.

The rock-hard perch of his thighs only added to the spiraling heat. The equally solid length of his arousal nudged her abdomen, gave her no quarter in that direction either.

Not that she wanted any. The man provided an erotic cradle for her hips, along with the growing knowledge things were only going to get hotter.

"I want to touch you, too." She splayed her hands across his chest, absorbed the rapid pulse of his heart through the gray cotton of his dress shirt.

Sliding her fingers under his suspenders, she nudged them off his shoulders the way she'd wanted to all week, then tackled the shirt buttons. She worked her way down while he worked his way up, and when they met in the middle, Greg shrugged his way out of the sleeves.

And unveiled the sexiest chest she'd seen in all her life.

She'd encountered plenty of good-looking guys at the beach every summer, but Greg put them all to shame. Who knew Joe Corporate would be hiding the lean wiry muscle of a pro swimmer?

She whistled her appreciation under her breath and then collapsed into him, pressing herself to him in a delicious meld of soft curve to rock-hard pecs. Gripping the leather headrest behind Greg with both hands, she arched forward to rub herself across him, to graze his body with hers in a long, sinuous stretch.

Greg hissed out a breath between clenched teeth. A thrill tripped through her that she could spark such a reaction in him.

Before she could position herself for another pass over his body, however, he rose out of the chair, bringing her with him.

"You're not nearly naked enough yet," he growled just before he brought his lips down to hers again. His tongue teased hers, stroked her, made her desperate for more of him.

He answered her restless moans by pulling the drawstring cord of her khakis and dipping one hand beneath the waistband.

She'd never committed so much to a man before. She was now well beyond the point of anything she'd ever done in her past. No man had ever touched the satin front of her panties before. The guys in college had seemed little more than boys. And her life since then had been all about writing music and lyrics, singing songs and perfecting her craft.

Now she knew why.

She'd simply been waiting for the man with the most perfect touch ever.

He cupped his palm around her, hugging her as snugly as her new pink thong.

Any thought of college guys or past second-base experiences vanished from her mind. She could only concentrate on the extraordinary pleasure wrought by that single, delicious caress.

Greg's heart hammered against hers, his breath hot in her hair and on her neck. "Are you sure about this?" he whispered in the acoustically perfect room. "About *here?*"

She whimpered at the delay. "I can't wait for anywhere else."

Like a genie granting all her wishes, Greg made Jackie's khakis disappear. His trousers and boxers followed in quick succession, leaving her only a moment to admire the shadowed view of his naked body before he backed her against the clear glass of the sound studio's door.

He braced himself with one hand on the door on either side of her head, her shoulders bracketed by flexed biceps.

Oh my.

Jackie had always been a take-charge kind of woman, but just now, she was only too happy to indulge this erotic display of masculine dominance. She licked her lips, undeniably aroused.

His erection pressed against her belly. He reached down to stuff a foil packet in her palm, no doubt taken from his pants in some sleight of hand when he'd made their clothes disappear.

"You're calling the shots," he assured her in spite of his muscles pressing her body exactly where he wanted her at the moment. "Use this whenever you're ready."

Her fingers fumbled with the package. She would have used her teeth on the damn thing if it hadn't given way at the last second.

Desire made her tremble, tingle. She rolled the condom over him with all the finesse of a first-timer, but Greg didn't seem to notice. He was too busy licking her neck, nibbling her ear, and kissing a heated path to her breasts, distracting her all the more.

No sooner had she completed her task than he lifted her off the floor, guiding her legs around his hips.

Grateful she'd spent all week swinging from vines and trees, Jackie easily locked her ankles behind him and held on for all she was worth. Clinging to Greg De Costa was an erotic treat she'd never, ever forget.

His arousal nudged the sweet spot between her thighs, assuring her she was more than ready for this foray into sexual experience. In fact, if she didn't feel him inside her this minute, she'd explode with the want of him.

She reached between them to stroke him with one hand, shamelessly enjoying the fierce stiffening of his whole body at that lone touch.

He shifted her against the door, steadied her hips with his hand and guided himself inside her. Slowly.

Jackie tensed, gripped his shoulders against the slight sting that came in conjunction with intense pleasure.

"Are you okay?" he whispered, his voice filled with a tenderness she hadn't expected.

She nodded. But until he ran a gentle finger over her mouth, she hadn't realized she'd been biting her lip.

Taking a deep breath, she braced herself for the rest of him. Instead of plunging forward, Greg reached between them to touch her, drawing tight circles around her center of sensation and calling forth a quivering, breathless wave of sweet heat.

Only then, when she teetered on the brink of something utterly luscious, did he ease himself the rest of the way inside. Any pain she might have felt melted beneath the continued manipulation of his fingers.

She looked up at him, her eyes open with the wonder of new experience, and found his gaze on her. In that brief moment, she saw that he knew her secret, recognized that her virginal status had been detected.

Not that she owed him an explanation.

Her body was hers to give where she chose.

And judging from the waves of liquid sensation

shooting through her, Jackie knew she'd chosen very wisely.

They kissed, clung, moved together like they'd been lovers for years. Or so it seemed to Jackie. Greg anticipated her every need, drawing her over and over again to that point of seductive drowning, only to pull her back at the last moment.

Finally, she utilized her skills as a jungle woman, gripping his waist with her thighs and locking his body to hers. She could sense his loss of control, felt his ruthless restraint as he touched her most sensitive spot one last time until he called forth the magic she wanted.

She couldn't help the cry that escaped her lips as she hurtled into the sea of pulsing sensation. One long, perfect note hummed through her, but this was no tame middle C. The glorious fulfillment Greg gave her sent her into an octave range she'd never even touched before.

She felt the arch of his own body moments after hers, knew his satisfaction has been as complete as her own.

Their breathing, their hearts beating filled the room. The misty fog covering all the windows grew all the more dense in the wake of their lovemaking. Jackie couldn't imagine how she could ever pry herself loose of this man.

Greg backed them into one of the leather chairs and cradled her to his chest, still locked together. Her ankles had come unhitched so that her thighs folded neatly against his.

She knew sex wasn't supposed to make her turn into

a romantic dreamer. She'd talked to enough girlfriends to know sex could create an illusion of closeness that didn't really exist.

But for these few moments, Jackie let herself pretend this feeling of total completeness could last. That Greg wouldn't make a big deal about the whole virgin thing.

And that she would remember the wild man she'd shared her body with tonight even when he turned back into the smooth-talking, straight and narrow corporate guy tomorrow.

9

GREG STRUGGLED TO STEEL himself against the hypnotic rise and fall of Jackie's breath along his shoulder, the seductive invitation of her cinnamon hair draped across his chest like a blanket.

At some point, Jackie had eased back into her panties and had tossed his boxers across his lap, but other than that, they remained mostly naked and strewn across the leather chair.

Everything about the moment begged him to relax, to enjoy, to indulge himself in the quiet aftermath of the best sex he'd ever had in his life.

Except that he'd created said moment with a *virgin*.

A commotion-causing, scene-stealing, Zing-O-Gram girl his friends had all seen naked, but a virgin nevertheless. The notion boggled the mind. Humbled him to his toes.

And reminded him with every soft huff of CO_2 over his chest that he needed to have a serious conversation with the woman in his arms. The sex that should have been sort of simple had somehow become monumental by the sheer magnitude of the gift she'd given him.

"Jackie?" He shifted her weight on his lap.

For a moment, he thought she'd fallen asleep. Even after she stirred enough to look up at him, her movements were soft and languid. Only her green eyes were alert, wary.

"What?" A furrow creased her brow, centered squarely over her nose.

The directness of her gaze made him second-guess his strategy. He'd never been super in-tune to feminine emotions, but with straightforward Jackie, Greg didn't need to have a master's in women's studies to read her mood.

He tried another tact, unwilling to tamper with their tentative connection just yet.

"What will you do now that we've wrapped the commercial shooting?" He stroked her hair, telling himself he wanted to put her at ease, knowing he would have used any excuse to keep touching her. "I mean, how does one go back to freelance copywriting after tackling a role like Tarzan's Jane?"

Slowly the furrowed brow disappeared.

She reclined against him, gently kicking the mixing board with one foot to send their chair spinning in a lazy half circle. She felt so damn good next to him. What made a woman save herself for twenty-four years, only to spend her first time on a raucous encounter in a sound studio?

With a guy like Greg, no less?

Seemingly unaware of his inner turmoil, Jackie thought about his question for a moment before answering.

"Admittedly, copywriting isn't exactly musical composing, but it's not bad."

"That's what you want to do long-term? Compose music?"

She stiffened for a moment as if he'd somehow unearthed a big secret. But then her body relaxed and she kicked the edge of the mixing board again to send them in a half spin in the opposite direction.

"Yes. I'm going to build to it slowly because I don't want to follow the same route as my parents, but that's where I'd like to get eventually."

Obviously, Jackie had issues with her supersuccessful musical family. Greg patted himself on the back for having been paying attention. Maybe he'd really matured since his relationship with the meteorologist and he'd be able to figure out women this time around.

"You don't want to cash in on their success to get a leg up in your own career," he clarified, certain he was going to be able to think this through despite the way the walls were spinning around him. "Sort of like a show of independence."

"Not exactly. My mom and dad are serious composers and I'm the kazoo, harmonica and cymbal player, remember?"

She sent them on yet another spin, launching Greg into definite dizzy terrain. Why had he thought he might be able to keep up with this woman?

He planted his feet more firmly in the industrial carpet and brought their careening world to a halt. "Meaning you want to compose piccolo solos and symphonies for the ukulele?"

"No. I'm just saying I'd like to write a much different

style of music than they have. If I tried to follow their path, I think there would be a lot of people who'd be disappointed by what I have to offer because it's so different from what my parents have done." She contented her restless feet to playing with Greg's discarded shoes. She tried them on, peered down at their clunky weight on her small feet and then slipped them back off again. "And let's face it, no one wants to be a letdown."

There was probably a message in there, but his brain was still back on the kazoo. He'd never cut it in women's studies. "So what *do* you want to compose?"

"Commercial music. Fun lyrics you can sing to, jingles that stay in your head for hours, and maybe one day..."

"What?"

"Never mind. You'll probably think I seduced you for a foot in the door."

He lifted her chin with one hand, urged her to look straight into his eyes. "I know the cat suit thing was an accident, Jackie. I just went into high-anxiety mode because of a relationship I had with a meteorologist here at the station. She ended up using her position to take jabs at me, but I know you'd never do that."

And he did. He hadn't fully realized it until he'd declared the words, but he stood behind the sentiment. Jackie had been the consummate professional on the set all week, never so much as alluding to their first meeting in front of anyone on the crew.

She nodded. "Thanks for that. And my dream is to compose for television shows at some point, maybe even a movie soundtrack one day." She whispered the last part, as if afraid to jinx her secret wish. "But I won't submit my ideas to anyone at WBCI for a while. I promise not to trade on my prominent connection here."

Winking up at him, she levered herself out of the chair and moved to retrieve her tank top.

Greg had more to say to her, but he lost the thread of his thoughts in an effort to steal a last glimpse of her generous curves before she covered them up again.

He scrambled for his pants before his body got any ideas about a second go-round tonight. She'd been a virgin.

Virgin.

Maybe if he repeated the word often enough he'd get it through his head.

"Jackie?" He zipped his pants and went to work on buttoning his shirt, determined to discuss the whole first time thing. He'd be an insensitive jerk *not* to say anything about it, wouldn't he? "We need to talk."

She tied the drawstring on her khakis and turned to face him. Flinging her denim jacket over one arm she looked more ready to flee than converse. "We do?"

He left his shirt buttons undone and reached for her, steering her into the leather chair that wasn't strewn with his tie and suspenders.

"Yes. We do." He sat across from her, studying her expression for a hint of recognition. Wasn't it obvious what he wanted to discuss?

Forsaking all pretense that he knew how to play Joe Sensitive for her, Greg launched straight to the heart of the matter. "Damn it, Jackie, if I'd known it was your first time, we could have found a bed."

Her jaw dropped.

Greg couldn't help thinking if he'd managed to shock Jackie, he'd probably really overstepped his bounds. "That is—"

"Let's be honest at least, since we are being forthright." She clutched her jacket with both hands as if she wanted to throttle it.

Greg had the distinct impression she wished *he* was the recipient of her white knuckled grip.

"If you'd known it was my first time," she continued, her gaze never leaving his, "nothing would have happened tonight."

She had him there.

If Greg had any clue about her untouched status, he would have let her seek a more worthy candidate for such an all-important "first." But after the unconventional way they'd met—what with her clothes falling off and all—he would have never guessed.

His image of her continued to shift and change as he learned more about her. First, she'd proven herself to be the ultimate professional on the set—something he'd never expected from a woman who confused a bachelor party for a six-year-old's birthday party. Her level of commitment to her work matched his own.

And now, she'd completely called into question his impression of her as an unconventional free spirit by revealing something semi old-fashioned and utterly charming.

She'd been saving herself.

He wanted to ask, why me?

But that might be a question she wasn't prepared to answer. So he settled for something simpler and less direct.

"Can you at least tell me why now? Why tonight?"

JACKIE COULD PRACTICALLY hear the wheels turning behind Greg's intent brown eyes.

She'd been two minutes away from escaping this conversation and the intimacy of the sound studio, but Greg had a knack for pinning her down and making her confront sticky situations.

She would simply keep this discussion light. She might have been saving it up for twenty-four years, but that didn't mean she owed any great explanation to the man who'd saved her from self-imposed celibacy.

"I thought if I was giving lessons in seduction to Hannah, I'd better get some practical experience myself. Didn't you tell me you wouldn't want me to teach her incorrectly?"

"You'll shock the braids right out of her hair if you share any information you picked up tonight, Jackie. Somehow I doubt Mike's going to treat Hannah to a first time in a soundbooth." He stuffed his tie in one shirt pocket and his suspenders in the other.

Jackie's gaze lingered on the open V of his half-buttoned shirt. Those lean swimmer's muscles made her mouth water despite the uncomfortable conversation. Her body ached just a little from their first time, but not enough that she wouldn't be interested in a second time.

"Maybe he should," Jackie argued, partly to be contrary and partly to seize any topic besides her recently breached virginal status. "Every woman appreciates a little spontaneity."

"Some more than others." Greg cast her a pointed look. "So you decided tonight was a good night because you have to tutor someone in seduction?"

If he expected her to say she'd chosen tonight because she was head over heels for him, he was bound to be disappointed.

Okay, maybe she liked him a lot more than she should, but she was still smart enough to know Greg De Costa couldn't be any more wrong for her. He probably spent every Saturday sitting on charity boards and every Sunday catching up on work, while Jackie firmly believed in fun for fun's sake. Art for art's sake and not as a means to get ahead in life.

"I decided tonight was a good night because my twenty-fifth birthday is in two weeks and I couldn't bear to enter my second quarter century with my hymen intact, okay? It's not really something I want to talk about."

Had she imagined the flash of hurt in his eyes? Judging by the disgruntled scowl she saw of his expression, she probably had.

"I don't think you're taking this seriously enough."

She recognized a stage cue when she heard one, and that direction couldn't have been more clear if it had been written in lights.

This was her moment to exit.

She rose. "Maybe that's because you seem to be taking things seriously enough for both of us." Her feet strayed toward the door, but she found she had more to say. Frustration churned through her.

"I can handle being a professional on the job, Greg, but I can't be Ms. No-Nonsense after hours, too. I can't be serious all the time." She reached for the door, really wishing she could just make her big exit and get out of here.

This time, Greg foiled the attempt by gently encircling her wrist with his fingers.

Something about his touch in the wake of what they'd shared tonight did soft, squishy things to her insides. Especially when his sudden proximity put her up close and personal to his unbuttoned shirt and all that sleek, lean muscle.

He leaned closer to speak quietly, his gaze seeming to see only her. "Jackie, you play a kazoo in your off-hours. I don't think anyone's going to accuse you of being serious all the time. I'm just wondering what tonight means for us and how things will play out between us once Monday rolls around."

And therein lay Greg's bottom line.

Monday.

He wanted to know how this would affect his work environment.

Jackie closed her eyes against the magnetic draw of steely pecs and opened the door to Studio A. "Monday we go back to being two professionals. I don't even need to be here when you screen the commercial. You can call me if Shamus decides he wants to produce the jingle as part of the soundtrack, and if he does, then I'll breeze in here the same way I have all week."

She plowed through the door and away from the conversation.

Greg followed in her wake, the clips of his suspenders jangling in his shirt pocket as he hurried to catch up to her. "You belong at that meeting Monday. Are you willing to sacrifice that moment of knowing you've done your job well just because you want to walk away from tonight like nothing even happened?"

What else did he expect her to do? Greg seemed unafraid to quiz her about her position on the confusing issue of their relationship, but had he bothered to share one iota of his own feelings with her?

"No." She wove between a couple of tripods with wheels and paused in front of the jungle set, gazing longingly at the vine she'd swung from all week. She wondered how Greg could have seen it hanging there day in and day out and not have tried it out.

The prop only reminded her why she didn't need another person in her life who wanted to censor her.

Her body still aching with the memory of Greg, Jackie took a deep breath and hoped she had gathered enough acting talent this week to deliver the line—the lie—this scene required.

"I'm just reassuring you that tonight doesn't change a thing for us."

DOESN'T CHANGE A THING?

Twelve hours later and those words still hurt Greg like hell. He unlocked the private skybox at Fenway

Park and wished he hadn't promised to meet Mike at today's Red Sox game. Baseball might be a cure-all for some guys, but sports had never been a magic mind-numbing elixir for Greg.

What he wanted was Jackie.

He pushed his way inside the living area of the luxury suite. One of the perks of working for WBCI was access to corporate amenities like this one. It wasn't super plush by more modern baseball park standards, but there was a sofa and love seat, three TVs in case you wanted to catch updates on other games, and a row of theater seating up front by the windows for when you wanted to pay full attention to the game.

A great setup for a handyman's son who'd worked his way up from the streets of South Boston.

Greg had busted his tail to be able to indulge in the perfect view from just above home plate. He opened the windows overlooking the field to catch the scents of hot dogs and to hear the noise of the crowd. The sun was shining and the Sox were playing their first home game against the Yankees. He should be having the time of his life today instead of continually replaying Jackie's simple summary of their night together....

Doesn't change a thing.

He poured himself a beer from the amply stocked refrigerator and wondered why she had to be so adamant about that. Did her first-time status blind her to how fantastic their night together had been?

After all, it wasn't every couple who generated the kind of sizzle they had. He'd like to think she'd be pretty damn disappointed if she ventured into an intimate relationship with anyone else and discovered as much for herself.

Not that he was in any hurry for her to find out.

At all.

The thought of her with anyone else brought with it a dose of jealousy Greg couldn't recall feeling about any other women.

The door to the skybox opened before he could think about Jackie's retreat any further. His brother stepped halfway inside, wearing a Red Sox jersey and smiling as big as if he were going to throw out the first pitch.

"Hey, Greg," he called, still holding the door open. "You wouldn't care if I asked Hannah to join us today, would you?"

"Of course not." Greg would just have to play third wheel the day after Jackie told him their night together didn't mean a damn thing to her. He'd get over it. "Hannah's practically family."

Mike leaned into the corridor and pulled Hannah inside. He didn't let go of her once he'd steered her inside either, opting instead to keep his hand on the small of her back.

Both of them smiled ear-to-ear.

Greg hazarded a guess that Jackie's seduction lessons had paid off in spades. At least someone was smiling today.

"Hi, Greg." Hannah waved at him, her single blond braid tucked through the hole in the back of her baseball cap. She looked around the skybox for all of two seconds before asking, "Where's Jackie?"

He passed a bottle opener to his brother and gestured toward the refrigerator so that Mike would help himself.

"I'm not sure what her plans were today." He hadn't thought to invite her to the game once he realized she was ready to write off their night together as no big deal. "We're going to talk on Monday after I show our commercial to the client."

He still couldn't believe she wasn't going to attend the screening.

Mike and Hannah exchanged a split-second look that only lovebirds could interpret apparently.

"What?" If that look had been about *him*, he wanted to know. "You think I should have asked her here?"

Jackie would have only cut him off at the knees anyway. Wouldn't she?

Mike handed Hannah a beer while the two of them shrugged in unison.

Hannah sank into one of the couches. "It's just that Jackie seems like a baseball kind of girl. She'd probably have more fun hanging out at Fenway for the day than going to all the benefits and black-tie stuff you normally end up doing on the weekend."

Greg frowned, seeing her point. He'd be willing to bet Jackie refused all black-tie invites on principle alone.

Hannah hopped back up, braid swinging. "I'm going to go call her as long as I won't be seeing her here today." She cast a mildly censorious look in Greg's direction, then winked at Mike as she headed for the door. "She'll want to know what a good student I made."

Greg was surprised to see his brother, a lady charmer from way back, flush at her words.

Nevertheless, his grin returned in full force.

As Hannah shut the door behind her, Greg tossed a pack of beer nuts at Mike's chest. "I take it the wedding's back on?"

Mike tore open the package and dropped into a front row seat. "I've been too afraid to ask, but it looks good after last night. I'm not going to ask about it until I'm ready to re-propose and the whole bit."

"Since when did you turn into Joe Romance?" Greg claimed a seat two down from his brother and focused on the player coming up to plate for the first at bat of the game.

"Since I practically lost the love of my life, bro. Get a clue." Mike tossed back a handful of nuts and then threw one squarely into Greg's temple. "Speaking of which, you look to be mucking up another relationship early in the game."

Greg winged the nut back at Mike. He took no pleasure in his between-the-eyes hit, however. Why'd Mike have to bring up Jackie? Greg had almost gone three minutes without thinking about her or her decision to give him the most precious gift she'd ever given any man.

Almost.

"I am *not* taking advice from my little brother who almost lost his fiancée, so we don't need to go there."

Mike whistled loud and long as the pitcher struck out the first batter. "Just seems to me you're probably not giving Jackie a fair shake after all the hoopla the weathergirl caused."

"She almost cost me my job, Mike. I know that wouldn't faze you, but it scares the hell out of me." He'd been poor once, and he was never going to revisit those days. No matter how much money he socked away for a rainy day, he never wanted that rainy day to arrive. "I've got one career field and I want to stay in it."

"Sure seemed to me like you were having a good time playing director on the set last week." He paused to watch a pop fly go foul into the stands. "It's been a few years since you've been behind a camera."

"When you move up, you move away from the camera." Besides, the prestige of his job made up for not being able to exercise his interest in production, didn't it? "I'm perfectly happy where I am, and I'm not going to screw that up again just because I seem to be attracted to the zaniest women Boston has to offer."

Mike cheered for a guy in the stands who caught a second fly ball. "You're right. Jackie's a reformed stripper, after all. She's probably got quite the track record for leading guys astray."

Greg knew Mike was yanking his chain. Hannah and Jackie had seemed to hit it off so well that both Hannah and Mike must realize Jackie had never been a stripper.

Still, his brother's comments made him wonder if he'd been out of line last night trying to pin her down about what she wanted. And maybe he wasn't giving her a fair chance because of how close he'd come to ruining his career with a spectacularly failed relationship.

How could he expect her to know what she wanted out of their mutual attraction when he couldn't begin to guess what *he* wanted?

Damn.

He needed to talk to her. Now.

Greg rose from his seat and left his barely touched beer on a tray by the door. "I'm taking off, Mike, but hang out as long you want."

Mike flashed a thumbs-up sign over one shoulder. "Go get her, tiger."

Damn straight he would go get her.

Greg adjusted his tie as he went out the door. He'd never encountered a problem, a task or a woman that he couldn't solve, complete or charm. And Jackie Brady, for all her harmonica-playing, whisker-wearing disregard for convention would be no different.

As long as she didn't distract him by running around in a suede bikini or dropping her cat costume, he'd be fine.

10

Jackie closed her eyes against the bright April sun, allowing strains of *Peter and the Wolf* to float over her. She had fled her apartment this morning, seeking the relative solitude of her brownstone's communal backyard.

She loved working outdoors in warm weather and she soaked up the sun like a Hawaiian Tropic girl in an orange polka dot bikini that had seen better days. As long as she wore her SPF-15, she felt entitled to a tan.

Since she'd never liked the fussy wrought iron table and chairs near an old fashioned birdbath, she'd bought a classic American picnic table and stained it in redwood. Whenever life felt too busy or too daunting, she sought out her picnic table and some fickle Boston sunshine to work on her musical scores or to just be creative.

Today she'd needed to escape thoughts of black leather armchairs, a steamy sound studio and a certain stud in suspenders.

Her trick might have worked if she'd at least been able to sing her new songs. But she'd awakened feeling too guilty about her night with Greg to test out her new—and potentially more intense—vocal powers. In the gentle light of day it seemed sort of crass to have rationalized intimacy with a man for something so self-serving as improving her art.

So she listened to *Peter and the Wolf* and ignored her own children's musical piece sitting half-finished in her lap. She'd been working on a composition that was sort of like a mini-operetta with a comic premise about a dancing hippo, but she couldn't write the words if she couldn't sing the music. And she couldn't sing because she felt too guilty that she might have used Greg.

Of course, the more acutely scary thought keeping her from working was that she hadn't used Greg at all. Deep inside, she feared she'd given herself to him last night simply because she'd wanted *him*.

And if that were true, she had the feeling her heart was headed for big trouble.

For one thing, Greg would never forsake his big-time place in the media world to hang out with a woman who thrived on commotion. And for another, she knew that even if she tried to tame her ways to please someone else, she'd only end up disappointing that person.

If life in the Brady household had taught her anything, it was that she needed to be true to herself. She'd rather disappoint people being Jackie Brady than to be miserable trying to fit someone else's mold for her.

Of course, knowing that didn't help her figure out what to do about Greg or tell her how to make music from this morning's case of heartache.

An insistent chirping noise began to blend with *Peter and the Wolf*. She turned the music down only to realize her phone was ringing three floors up. Again.

Apparently someone really wanted to talk to her today.

Telling herself she was only curious that it might be work related and not that she was dying to know if Greg had been trying to reach her, Jackie headed for the side entrance of her brownstone.

She almost tripped over her own feet when she nearly plowed into a male chest clothed in a white oxford with red-and-blue suspenders decorated with Red Sox logos. Slowly, she looked up into the heated dark eyes that had teased her through her dreams the whole previous night.

"Greg." She didn't know quite what else to say, but she didn't move an inch, couldn't back away from the magnetic draw of a body she'd had the pleasure of getting to know oh-so-well.

He didn't seem too ready to talk either, judging by his silent assessment of her.

"Greg?" She wiped her hand back and forth in front of his rapt gaze, afraid if she didn't pry those intense eyes off her half-clad body, she was going to wind up in a repeat performance of last night before too long.

"You're wearing a bathing suit." His voice slid along her senses as he stated the obvious.

She might as well have been naked for the immediate shock of awareness that cruised through her at his perusal. Jackie took deep breaths, unprepared to tread back into dangerous terrain with this man. She hadn't fully recovered from their first round—emotionally at least. Physically, her body seemed to already be drifting closer to his.

"I know it's a huge beauty sin to worship the sun these days, but I think I'm part lizard because I love to just plaster myself to a rock and allow those rays to heat me right up." She babbled shamelessly, thinking if she could keep her mouth busy talking she couldn't possibly kiss him.

Or so she hoped.

He nodded, dragging his gaze upward to meet hers. "You know, threat of skin damage aside, it might be nice if you put on a shirt so I can at least talk to you."

She frowned in an effort to follow his thinking.

"Frankly, I get a little distracted around you when you're half-naked, Brady, and what I need to say is too important to screw up because I'm busy ogling you."

He cast her a grin that could have sold ice to an Eskimo.

A female Eskimo, anyhow.

She nearly melted right at the man's feet. Knowing that he found her body distracting, maybe even a little enticing, incited alternating chills and tingles from her eyelashes to her toenails.

"Can we go inside?" He pointed toward the side entrance.

Nodding, she pointed toward the backyard. "Let me just grab my stuff first."

He followed her to the picnic table, scooping up her CD player once she'd hit the off button. Although not, apparently, before he noticed what she'd been listening to.

"I thought you weren't a classical musical fan." He waited while she picked up her notebook and pencil.

She could sense the heat in her cheeks, knew she was probably blushing as if she'd been caught committing a crime. Damn her transparent self.

"It's children's music," she offered as a weak rebuttal, fleeing toward the side entrance of the brownstone. "That's different."

He said nothing as he held the door for her and quietly followed her up the first flight of stairs. She had no choice but to fill the silence.

"When you think about it, there really aren't enough songs like 'Peter and the Wolf' and 'Flight of the Bumblebee.' Kids love that sort of stuff." She confronted him in the middle of the second flight of stairs. "Don't you think?"

He smiled up at her with perfect teeth and wind-blown hair. "You're writing classical music for kids on the sly, aren't you?"

She felt her jaw drop. She couldn't close it again, even knowing her expression was confirming his wild guess. Instead, she marched up the rest of the stairs in mild shock.

He didn't tease her with his new knowledge however, or try to convince her there was no money or prestige in creating classical music for kids. He merely caught up to her at the top of the stairs and fell into pace beside her.

"It sounds fun." He paused at the door of her third-floor apartment and waited while she unlocked the dead bolt. "And I bet you're great at it. Care to tell me why you keep it a secret?"

She struggled to find her conversational footing as

they entered her apartment. Wasn't it enough that Greg had shaken up her personal life? Now he had to charge headlong into the secret dreams of her professional life as well.

"It's not really a secret," she lied, fully aware there wasn't another soul who knew what she worked on in the sanctity of her backyard haven. "I'm probably light years away from achieving that goal. And it's not like I don't want to write my commercial jingles, because I do. I just see the kids' music as something pretty far down my career path, so I don't really talk too much about it."

Hadn't she bared enough of herself to this man in the studio?

Desperate to put the topic behind her, Jackie set her papers on a curio table and gestured toward an overstuffed lounger. "Why don't you have a seat and I'll go get dressed?"

PRIMITIVE MALE INSTINCT urged Greg to follow Jackie into her bedroom and tell her not to bother getting dressed. A *very* primitive male urge had a great deal of fun with that fantasy for at least thirty seconds after she disappeared down the yellow, sponge-painted hallway.

But he wasn't here to act on instinct.

Greg wanted Jackie. Not just for the afternoon, but for many, many afternoons. And nights. And weekends. He wanted to take a chance for the first time since his former girlfriend had plastered his face all over the evening news with a big X across his mug.

Sure, seeing Jackie would be risky. She did have that penchant for making a scene, but it wasn't like she consciously tried to draw attention to herself. She simply possessed the kind of vibrant personality that couldn't help but be expressive. A fact her brightly colored apartment attested to with its coral walls in the living room and a kitchen wallpapered in apples and watermelons.

Greg appreciated her exuberant personality on a personal level. And he could accept it on a professional plane. Now that their commercial work together would be drawing to a close, it's not like their professional paths would be crossing. If they did, it wouldn't be any time too soon.

With a little effort, Greg could hold on to his publicly visible position and still follow his attraction to an offbeat, high-profile woman. Something about Jackie inspired the creativity he had to stifle in his current job, fed a need he'd allowed to lapse for too long.

Besides, the more time he spent with her, the more he wanted to learn about this complex woman with the power to make him smile.

She emerged in frayed denim shorts and a white T-shirt with the name of a Newbury Street bar emblazoned across the front. How did she still look so good in clothes that could have been Mike's castoffs?

On a whim, he asked, "You want to take in the Red Sox game?" Hadn't Mike and Hannah said Jackie was the kind of woman who would appreciate a day of baseball?

Hard to believe a sexy songbird who grew up in the lap of luxury would enjoy America's pastime.

She looked down at her clunky wristwatch. "It's probably already in the sixth inning. I don't think there'd be much left to see by the time we drove over there."

So he was a little impressed that she knew when the Sox played.

But then, maybe Jackie wouldn't enjoy the isolated experience of watching a game from a luxury suite. Perhaps she was the kind of woman who would rather party in the stands with the rest of the crowd and participate in the funky chicken during the seventh inning stretch.

He'd never met a woman so full of contradictions.

She watched him, smiling. "Is that why you dropped by, Greg? To ask me to the game?"

Showtime.

He couldn't have asked for a better opening. Now he only needed to find the right words to convince her to give him a chance.

"I have a proposition for you." Damn. How had this already ended up sounding like a business deal? "Actually more of a personal scheme."

She nodded as if she understood him perfectly even though the perplexed look in her green eyes told him otherwise.

He was about to suggest they sit down at the fifties-style diner table tucked in a breakfast nook so he could make a proper pitch for himself when she asked, "Lemonade?"

The woman had a knack for keeping him on his toes.

"Okay," he responded, following her into the water-melon-and-apple patterned kitchen. "But are you try-ing to distract me?"

She smiled over the refrigerator door as she pulled out a heavy glass pitcher full of lemon slices and ice cubes. "Maybe. You're looking awfully serious."

Something Jackie Brady didn't respond well to, of course. He'd learned that the hard way last night.

Greg took a deep breath and tried not to think like a high-level manager. Too serious.

Time to draw on the creative side of his brain—his long-shelved production skills. While Jackie poured two glasses of lemonade, he blocked this scene in his mind and tried to think how he'd stage it if he were be-hind a camera.

The whole thing unfolded plain as day.

And it started with plucking the pitcher from Jackie's hand.

"What?" She looked up at him, green eyes wide and startled.

Perhaps she saw a hint of "the plan" in his gaze, be-cause her lips parted as he stepped closer. Her breath caught in her throat as he backed them up against the counter and then braced his arms on either side of her.

She smelled like sunshine and coconut oil—exactly like her commercial counterpart, Jane, ought to smell.

"If you're trying to distract me, Jackie, I can think of more surefire methods."

Her thighs shifted restlessly between his. One knee

grazed the inside of his leg. Just like that, she set him on fire.

She smiled with the knowing of Eve. An Eve offering lemons instead of apples.

"If I distract you that much, I might never find out what you came here for."

"Maybe *this* is what I came here for." He slanted his mouth to hers, allowing himself the pleasure of tasting her. Soft and slow, deliberately and thoroughly, he moved his lips over hers, coaxing her to let him inside.

She moaned her encouragement, a sweet, needy sound that made him realize he'd been missing her every minute since they'd walked out of Studio A last night. Those breathy little moans had filled his dreams and replayed in his waking fantasies.

He spanned her waist with his hands, molded her lithe dancer's body with his palms. She quivered under his fingertips.

His tongue tangled with hers, then stroked her lower lip until she arched into him. His fingers found their way to the nape of her neck, tracing light patterns on the sensitive skin there before he gathered up her cinnamon hair in one hand and gently tugged her head back to expose the long column of her neck.

He opened his eyes to absorb the view, greedily soaking in the sight of the blue vein jumping in her neck, the chill bumps just under the collar of her T-shirt and disappearing behind her shoulder.

Greg kissed the throbbing blue vein, following the path of that tiny line down to the hollow of her throat. Her hand fluttered against his chest, then clung to one suspender as if it might anchor her in the rising tide of heat that threatened to dominate the kitchen.

"I want you Jackie," he whispered the words as he kissed his way toward her ear and gently nipped the lobe. "If it's not too soon."

She opened her eyes and blinked up at him. "Too soon?"

He cupped her cheek in one hand while he shifted his other to curve around her waist, his thumb stroking the silky soft skin under her T-shirt.

"Since last night was a first," he explained, knowing he had the willpower to make himself stop touching her but praying he didn't have to. "I don't want to hurt you if it's too soon."

She shook her head with so much vehemence he had to smile.

"It will only hurt me if you stop," she whispered back, venturing one hand between their bodies to steal along the leather of his belt, then edged even lower...

Greg sucked in a breath to steel himself. For about three-quarters of a second it occurred to him that he was failing his primary mission miserably. He hadn't meant for a single kiss to sizzle so far out of control, but apparently he'd underestimated the firepower of Jackie Brady.

And then he couldn't think about his blasted mission anymore.

Just keeping himself in check throughout Jackie's increasingly adventurous caresses required every last bit of concentration he could scavenge.

Jackie watched in rapt fascination as Greg's jaw

tensed and flexed in time to the least little movement of her hands along the ridge below his belt.

Hungry for more of him, anxious to push him to his limits, she reached for his zipper and carefully tugged it down.

She hadn't progressed two inches southward when his hand gripped her wrist in a vise.

"Honey, you don't know what you're doing to me." His voice held a ragged edge, a dangerous note that tripped through her, thrilling every nerve ending along the way.

"Does it feel like I don't know what I'm doing?" she asked, nudging that zipper just a little farther with a rebellious finger.

He hissed out a breath between his teeth. "I know *you* don't mind making a scene. But I've got a problem with causing a stir, and let me tell you, it's going to be a hell of a note if I lose control right here in the damn kitchen of all places."

"Don't you ever give up control?" She continued to reach for him with her imprisoned hand, shameless for a chance to rattle his cage just a little.

He spread her arms wide and held them there, removing the barriers of their limbs from between them. Slowly, he grazed his body with hers, nudged her belly with the hard length of him that she had teased just a moment ago.

She went soft and warm inside, gladly sinking into the taut strength of him.

"I'll let you be on top," he offered, his gaze meeting

hers levelly. "That's all the compromise I can promise right now."

"That's enough for me." She ground her hips against his, too hungry for him to worry about who was in charge of this electric exchange. She licked her lips with a deliberate sweep of her tongue. "More than enough, in fact."

"Are you sweet-talking me?" He cupped her bottom with both hands and lifted her up against him. Jackie wrapped her legs around his waist to anchor herself. "Because if you are, I'm taking you to the bedroom and I'm going to demand some more."

He steered their way out of the kitchen, carrying her like a monkey glued to his side but with an erotic twist. Every step nudged the solid length of him against her most intimate parts, causing the sweet ache between her thighs to turn almost painful with want.

They half walked, half stumbled noisily across the hardwood floor in the living room and past the front door. They nearly fell into the locked door when a sharp knock sounded from the other side.

They froze, hearts pounding in fierce time together in the silence.

"Jacquelyn, darling, is that you?" Jackie's mother, the famous Deirdre Breslin Brady called through the thin wooden barrier. "Let us in, sweetheart, we've been shopping for your birthday."

Her father's voice—a flawless bass that had won awards the world over—rumbled low in perfect accompaniment to her mother's soprano.

"And have we got a surprise for you!"

11

Jackie was certain her parents couldn't have possibly purchased anything at Neiman Marcus that would rival the surprise Greg had been about to give her.

She might have simply not answered the knock given her overheated state, but she and Greg were so close to the door her parents could probably hear if Jackie and Greg so much as blinked.

With more than a little regret, Jackie slid off Greg and landed on the floor. Straightening her shirt, she leaned close to whisper in his ear, "Why don't you go pour more lemonade while I prep them?"

Not that Deirdre Breslin Brady would ever take so much as a sip of a drink so plebian as lemonade. She'd send it back to the kitchen with a request for chamomile tea, but at least the lemonade would give Greg something to do.

He flashed her a silent thumbs-up, but he didn't leave right away. He lingered in the foyer for a moment to drop a kiss against her throat and whisper back, "When they leave, you're all mine."

Warmth curled through her even as a second rap sounded against her door.

"Jacquelyn?" Both parental voices called in perfect harmony.

Taking a deep breath, she struggled to tamp down the desire still sparking through her. She pulled open the front door and prepared for the hurricane.

"Darling!" Niall and Deirdre entered the apartment the same way they'd entered any room throughout Jackie's life—as if they were celebrated movie stars during Hollywood's golden age.

Arms flung wide and public personas in place, they air-kissed her cheeks with synchronized smooches.

Deirdre marched past her daughter to fling herself on the sofa. Even on a warm spring day, she sported a floor-length black organza skirt and a red silk tank top printed with black African-inspired shapes.

The outfit was probably the most whimsical thing Deirdre owned—no matter that it was more dramatic than anything Jackie had worn in her entire life.

"You've no idea what the stores were like today, my love, but we simply had to find something appropriately lavish for our only child's twenty-fifth birthday."

Jackie caught a glimpse of Greg in the kitchen and searched for a way to interrupt as her mother chattered about Boston's never-ending traffic dilemmas.

Her father beat her to it, however, interrupting his wife to give Jackie a stern look. "Birthday shopping would have been much easier, Jacquelyn, if you could have just accepted your mother's tickets to young David Ormsby's concert next week."

He raised bushy dark eyebrows in the classic "haven't we talked to you about this, young lady" expression. Niall Brady had the deep-blue eyes of the Irish Sea and the wild dark hair of a young Orson

Wells. "He's been so eager to meet you ever since we told him about you—"

"No more musicians for me, Dad," Jackie returned, dreading a replay of the David Ormsby argument in front of Greg.

Especially since Greg had magically appeared the moment another man's name was mentioned, tray of glasses in hand.

"Lemonade anyone?"

Jackie would have been very sorry to see her parents taken down by whiplash, but she couldn't resist a giggle at their blatant rubbernecking to get a look at the new male in her apartment.

Utter silence followed Greg's inquiry.

She couldn't remember ever dating a man who hadn't been at least a little intimidated by her parents. Even the prodigy musicians her folks had set her up with had been scared silent in front of the famous duo.

But Greg charged forward to shake hands with both of them, looking utterly at ease despite the fact that he'd been carrying Jackie around the apartment with her legs glued to his hips not five minutes ago.

She knew on an intellectual level that she should feel relieved Greg turned on his I'm-head-of-the-local-network charm and had both her parents talking and laughing inside of two minutes.

Instead, she couldn't help but feel just a little left out as they compared notes on the world's most elite classical musicians.

As she watched Deirdre even make an effort to choke down a sip of the lemonade Greg had served,

Jackie realized how perfectly Greg would fit into their world. No matter where he was raised, he was a class act.

He probably wouldn't be caught dead with a kazoo in his mouth.

Perhaps realizing that Jackie hadn't been contributing to the conversation, Greg turned toward her. She'd lost the thread of what they'd been talking about since her brain had a habit of wandering whenever her father went on his monthly rant about the inferiority of local chamber music, a topic he'd broached with Greg a few moments earlier.

And she could tell by Greg's concerned expression he was going to drag her into the discussion.

"...but Jackie would know better since she's the composer," he began, deftly turning her parents' attention toward her as she attempted to fade into the coral-colored walls. "Jackie, wouldn't you say there is an increasing use of classical themes in commercial music?"

Her parents' gazes registered their shock.

Their tentative hope.

"You're composing again, Jacquelyn?" her father asked.

They reached for one another's hands on the sofa, as if by the strength of their combined wills they could make one unconventional daughter into the musical protégé of their dreams.

She had no choice but to disappoint them. Again.

Standing, she shook her head. "Nothing classical, only a few commercial jingles. I hate to rush you out, Mom and Dad, but Greg and I promised to meet some friends after the Red Sox game." She glanced at her watch with exaggerated surprise. "And look at the time! We really need to run."

Ignoring Greg's confused expression, she hustled her parents toward the door as much as anyone could hurry the Bradys. Her mother replaced her lemonade glass on the tray and hung up a garment bag from Neiman Marcus on the coatrack by Jackie's front door.

"It's a little something to wear in case you change your mind about the date with David. But then again, maybe you'll have an opportunity to wear it with Gregory," Deirdre whispered in Jackie's ear as the men shook hands. "And the other thing we wanted to give you," she began more loudly, peering over at Niall to be sure she had his attention.

"...is a birthday party!" They sang their big line in unison, increasing the impact with a tuneful delivery.

"Next Saturday out at the house, sweetheart," her father continued, leaning over his wife to kiss his daughter goodbye. "Gregory, you are most certainly invited. We'd love to see you there."

Jackie tried not to grind her teeth while Greg assured them he'd try his best to be there. She still couldn't believe he'd sold her out about her composing. He'd known she was writing on the sly, even if she hadn't fully admitted as much. So why the need to advertise the fact to her parents when she'd made it clear they were an impossible act to follow?

All of which she could have forgiven if she could be sure that Greg didn't care about appearances, that he was more concerned with what was inside than the superficial outside.

But as she watched him air-kiss Deirdre's cheek, she knew he could slide right into her parents confectionery world without missing a beat. Greg had ignored the production work he loved to take a job in the penthouse after all.

If she indulged her attraction to him, she'd only be subjecting herself to more rigid attitudes down the road. Sure, Greg liked her suede fringe bikini now. But she'd be willing to bet her furry cat costume he wouldn't want to be seen in public with such a nonconformist.

Even if she tried to change for him—and if anyone had ever tempted her to hang up her harmonica, it was this man—she knew her impulsiveness would explode free eventually. Probably in the middle of some important dinner.

Wouldn't it be better to bow out now, than to disappoint and embarrass him later?

GREG PATTED HIMSELF ON the back as he ushered Jackie's parents out the door. All things considered, the impromptu visit had gone pretty well.

And now that the illustrious Bradys had disappeared down the hall, he only had to shut the door and pick up where he left off.

Anticipation fired through him. The last half hour hanging out with Jackie's parents had nearly killed him. He'd scarcely been able to maintain a conversational thread because all he could think about was Jackie's legs wrapped around his waist.

Jackie's breathy sighs and questing fingers.

Jackie's soft breasts swaying against his chest...

Locking the door for privacy, Greg reached for her, only to discover she'd retreated halfway across the room.

Obviously he'd need to rebuild the atmosphere pre-Bradys. Perfectly understandable. A family reunion could douse the most persistent libido—except his apparently.

While he racked his brain to come up with the right approach, Jackie turned on him from her position on the other side of the living room.

"I don't think this will work." She made the declaration with arms folded and chin high.

He stepped closer, certain he must have misunderstood.

"That's close enough." She held out one palm in stop sign language. How could she have been so willing in his arms half an hour ago and still manage to look so fierce right now?

"If we get within touching distance of one another I'll only lose my train of thought," she explained, relaxing her arm at her side.

Her calf grazed the coffee table as she backed up a step. She steadied the lightweight maple piece and picked up a round coaster off the surface.

Confusion rocked him as he watched her flip the coaster over and over in one hand. No wonder all his attempts at relationships went awry. Even when he found a woman he wanted to be with, he couldn't begin to comprehend where she was coming from.

"I don't understand." He took a deep breath to clear his head, making a futile attempt to banish rogue sexual thoughts still flitting around his brain. This situation definitely required his full attention. In fact, maybe it required him to lay all his cards on the table. "I didn't come here today to woo you out of your clothes or anything like that, Jackie. I know we got sidetracked before your parents arrived, but all I really wanted today was to let you know I'd like to be with you more. Much more."

For a moment, he thought the direct approach might work. Jackie's mouth dropped open in a little "O" of surprise.

But before he could press his suit, she was already shaking her head.

"This thing between us," she pointed vaguely to the two of them. "It won't work, Greg."

His jaw dropped wide open.

"And you know this because the sex was sensational? Or maybe you're basing that on the fact that we work really well together?" Okay, so maybe that had come out a little sarcastic. But damn it, she had no reason to push him aside.

She shoved back a chair from her fifties-style diner table and dropped into the padded turquoise vinyl seat. Slapping the tiled stone coaster on the table, she met his gaze levelly.

"Actually, I know it won't work because I just saw how you were with my parents."

"You mean you saw how I can win over even the most intimidating people on the planet?" Greg tugged out a chair and sat around the corner from her, the shiny silver surface between them. Now he was in a venue he understood—face-to-face over a negotiating table. He could work with this. He *had* to. "I would think I'd have won points with that skillful layering on of charm."

Hadn't he just been patting himself on the back for smoothing things over with Deirdre and Niall?

"You fit right in." She confirmed his own impression, her face impassive.

"Isn't that a good thing?"

"I don't fit in, Greg. I never have." She traced her finger around and around the tiled coaster.

For a moment, he glimpsed a more vulnerable Jackie, a woman whose free spirit had been squelched too many times. Damn it, he would never want to do that to her.

"Seeing you with them made me realize how important 'fitting in' is to you. Your career depends on your ability to make nice with everyone—to be Joe Politically Correct. I thrive on ruffling feathers."

He barely knew where to begin refuting that argument. How could she be worried about something so minute?

"That's such a small facet of a relationship. I think it's something we can probably work around."

Again, she was shaking her head before he even finished his thought.

"It's not small to me. I've been a disappointment to

my parents—socially and professionally—more times than I can count. I'm not up for disappointing anyone else."

"I'd like to think I'm not that harsh of a judge—"

"I sing whenever I feel like it, Greg." She leaned closer, stabbing one unpainted fingernail down onto the table for emphasis. "And I've been known to carry a note even if it costs me my outfit. Can you honestly say you wouldn't be damn disappointed if I inadvertently embarrassed you at one of your big network television brouhahas?"

He took a second too long to answer. And hated himself for doing it.

Maybe he could have argued that he was busy envisioning her in that moment when her costume hit the floor at Mike's bachelor party and that's what slowed his response. But that wasn't fully the case.

He had been weighing the potential consequences of a relationship when he should have been dishing out an immediate denial.

Greg knew it. Worse, Jackie knew it.

"Jackie—"

"That's what I thought." A lopsided smile curved her soft lips.

After all the restless tracing and flipping of her drink coaster, Jackie laid the smooth tiled stone to rest on the table. Only then was Greg able to focus on the ardent couple embracing—hell, necking for all they were worth—painted on the tile.

If he hadn't screwed up the relationship negotiations big time, he might have been kissing Jackie like that even now. God, the thought of losing her was hurting way more than he'd ever expected.

"I think you're making me out to be a lot more strait-laced than I am," he countered, knowing she wouldn't be swayed but needing to make the point. He could be spontaneous too, damn it.

At the right time.

"It's not that I think you're straitlaced so much as just committed to your job. Your high-profile, have-to-keep-your-nose-clean job." She poked him in the suspender with one finger. "I understand better than you think."

Damn.

He didn't even know what to say to make things right. He'd been so certain he could win her over today, but he'd obviously come to the table unprepared.

Maybe all he needed was another chance. Another opportunity to see her.

"At least promise me you're going to show at the screening tomorrow," he nudged, seizing upon his one last chance for contact before she sang and tap danced her way right out of his life.

"I don't think—"

"It's my fault you didn't land that voice-over job when you should have, Jackie. Come to the screening and receive the kudos you deserve for your hard work." He studied her, rooting for a "yes" ten times harder than he'd ever willed the Sox into a win. Sure, the network execs were flying to Boston next week, but not until Thursday. By then, Jackie would be out of the

studio, and he'd have his head on straight again.
"Please."

He waited, hoped.

Slowly she nodded.

"Great. Thanks, Jackie." He rose abruptly to seal the
deal. If he didn't walk away from the table now, he'd
lose the important ground he'd just gained.

She stood too. "Then I guess I'll see you tomorrow."

Greg turned the doorknob to make his exit before
she changed her mind.

"But once we rake in the praise, I'm out of there."
She followed him to the door, looking at ~~him~~ with stern
green eyes and showing every inch of stubborn will
that seemed to make her a success at anything she ever
cared to try—whether it be singing, dancing, Zing-O-
Graming or composing. "No harm, no foul."

And no more relationship.

Yeah, he got the picture. That didn't mean he had to
agree with it.

To save him from making any promises he wouldn't
be able to keep, he simply winked.

SO SHE WAS A SUCKER.

As Jackie sat at the conference table on the sixth floor
of WBCI on Monday, she marveled at how easily Greg
had maneuvered her into showing up today.

You deserve the kudos, he'd said.

How could she—the woman who'd always had to
cause a commotion to command any attention—say no
to a legitimate opportunity to stand in the professional
spotlight for a few minutes? Of course she couldn't.

Even though Jackie was desperate to distance herself from Greg before she fell for him even more, she hadn't been able to stay away from the network today.

So she watched the final edit of the Back To Nature commercial in the darkened conference room, assuring herself she was only there out of professional pride and not because she secretly hoped to catch one last whiff of Greg's musky aftershave.

As Jackie's jingle music faded into silence, Greg flipped on the lights in the back of the room. She glanced across the table at Shamus for a hint of reaction, and was pleased to see him nodding his shaggy white head.

"Very, very nice." He smiled back at Greg and winked at Jackie. "The jungle theme is perfect. The jingle is outstanding. You're definitely on the right track."

On the right track?

Not exactly the kudos she'd hoped to receive on her first-ever national jingle.

Greg was already sliding into his seat at the head of the table, his expression concerned but not worried. And definitely not offended that Shamus had just given Greg's production efforts such faint praise. She wondered where Greg found the patience to deal with fickle clients.

"You don't think we're there yet?" Greg asked. He laced his fingers on top of his legal pad at the glass-topped conference table. "We had only planned to refine the soundtrack."

Shamus frowned, his lower lip curling downward

like a petulant child's. "It needs something else. More life. More verve."

He scratched his white head as if to massage the right answers from his brain. He scowled for so long that Jackie felt compelled to offer up the one idea she'd had from the beginning to improve the look of the commercial.

"Maybe it needs to be shot outdoors?" She knew Greg wouldn't approve—at least he hadn't seemed too thrilled the last time she'd mentioned it during their first night in Studio A—so she kept her gaze focused on Shamus.

Shamus snapped his fingers. "That's it," he practically shouted.

Jackie couldn't help but smile. If she'd wanted some professional affirmation today, Shamus's enthusiastic response had certainly provided as much.

Greg's voice, smooth and unruffled, wafted down the length of the long meeting table. "That's considerably more money, Shamus," he reminded his client. "And on top of what you've already spent on production it's going to skyrocket your costs right out of your budget."

Shamus stood, smiling and unfazed. "Didn't you want my business because I've got pockets deeper than the U.S. government, son? Let's reshoot it this week in a remote location. Something wild and natural. We need to have it ready by this weekend because I'm having a big party at my estate Saturday to unveil the new commercial. Invite whoever you'd like, by the way. The more the merrier."

Greg stood, looking a bit ruffled now despite his perfectly creased pants and his crisp shirt. He'd jammed a pencil behind one ear and practically sprinted around the conference table to catch up with his client.

"The rush job is going to cost even more, Shamus. And remote locations require a ton of equipment—"

Shamus clapped Greg on the shoulder. "Then spare no expense, son. Now, if you'll excuse me, I'm late for my tee time." He pointed at Jackie with a beefy finger on his way out the door. "Great job today, Ms. Brady. Thanks for the advice."

Jackie was probably beaming like a high-wattage bulb, but she couldn't seem to stop herself. Now that Shamus was having a big bash on the weekend, she had found the perfect excuse to politely extricate herself from her parents' birthday party plans. And not only that, but she'd managed to win a very rare dose of professional praise that would inspire her for weeks. Maybe she'd even find the creative energy to go home and write the ending to her dancing hippo operetta.

She had less than two seconds to enjoy her moment in the spotlight once Shamus walked out the door. Before she could fully bask in the glow of his commendation, Greg appeared before her, his dark eyes definitely not alight with the same good humor Shamus's had been.

"Congratulations." His tone of voice lacked the usual warmth that one conveyed with the sentiment. "Do you need me to recap what you've managed to accomplish here this morning? I've got network execs flying in from the West Coast this week, but instead of being in the office to meet them, I'll be out in Timbuktu filming Tarzan calls."

He took a step closer to her, the warm enticement of his body forcing her to take a step back.

"That also means that instead of wrapping up a production today, we've just signed on for a much longer, more complicated shoot. And since I'm the only producer Shamus will consider, that's all the more time I'll have to let my general manager duties slide." He stepped still closer, nudging Jackie back until her hip collided with the edge of the conference table.

"Yes, well—"

"Of course, since I'm no doubt lined up for a catastrophic fall from grace this week, I'm at least going to enjoy the fact that we are going to be in a *wild* and *remote* location for the taping." He stood perfectly still a hairbreadth from her, giving her every opportunity to remember exactly what it felt like to press her body against his, to lose herself in the heat and strength of him.

How did the man manage to make *wild* and *remote* sound like explicit sexual promises?

Maybe her on-location idea hadn't been the greatest.

"And since we'll be all alone in the middle of nowhere," Greg continued, "I hope you're prepared to encounter your share of temptation this week."

His warm breath against her cheek sent a shiver through her, a small tremble of anticipation she couldn't quite hide.

She couldn't have found enough voice to respond to his sensual threat if she tried. And she was definitely beginning to see the error of her ways today. Why hadn't she just allowed Shamus to come up with a solution for perfecting the commercial instead of consigning herself to more time—alone—with Greg?

She'd barely managed to send him away from her apartment yesterday, even though she had known it was the right thing to do. How would she be able to deny the rampant attraction between them when they would be rubbing elbows all week? She needed to be as quick and efficient as possible during their filming. The sooner she got her part over with, the sooner she could put Greg—and all the heady sensation he made her feel—behind her.

"Seems like you've made your bed," Greg whispered next to her ear, igniting chill bumps down her neck. "Now you'll have no choice but to lie on it." He grazed a thumb across the soft fullness of her mouth, nearly drawing a moan from her lips. "With me."

12

THE SILENCE ON LOCATION was deafening.

Greg never needed to call for "quiet on the set" because Jackie didn't seem to have a word to say to him on their shoot the next day. A few birds chirped the background noise, a few bees droned a warm spring sound, but other than that, the forest was still.

All Jackie's attention focused on the commercial and executing her part to perfection. Trouble was, she was so hyperfocused, she was coming across a bit stiff on camera.

He'd driven them in the WBCI location van to a secluded stretch of New Hampshire woods a couple of hours outside Boston. The remote locale would never pass for a jungle, but if Shamus wanted to reshoot the commercial in the Everglades next week, so be it. Greg had received permission to use the privately owned forest by fax last night, and he'd been assured he and Jackie wouldn't cross paths with another soul out here.

That was close enough to authentic for him.

Now all he needed to do was convince his Jane to get a little wild.

"Okay, Jackie, why don't you swing from the vine on the count of three? And make sure you really belt out the jungle cry. The audio is a little weaker out here with all the natural noises competing in the background."

Jackie nodded from her perch in a low-hanging oak branch, her toes brushing the leaves of a few skinny saplings as she swung her foot. Her brows furrowed in concentration. "Got it."

Apparently she'd talk to him about their work, she just didn't have much of anything else to say. She probably hadn't forgiven him for his not-so-subtle come-on after yesterday's meeting.

Could he help it if he'd been a little on the edge at the thought of spending days in total isolation with her? She'd given him the most titillating sex of his life—making him lose his cool to the point where he'd actually indulged himself in the workplace, of all things—and then she'd been prepared to walk away as if nothing had happened.

Of course he'd been rattled at the thought of going on location with her.

Alone.

He peered through the eyepiece of his camera and sized up her toned legs and symmetrical curves. She looked fantastic in her Jane outfit—sexy and appealing, but not so overt that she looked like a beer commercial.

Besides, something about her natural strength as she swung through the forest and perched on tree limbs gave her the don't-mess-with-me look that would appeal to the women in the audience.

"One, two..." Greg watched her grip the vine with

intense concentration and none of the usual restless energy that defined her movements. "Three."

Jackie swung out through the trees, her powerful launch sending her past her mark and inches from his camera lens.

Even the audio fell flat when her jungle cry sounded about as lively as a canned laugh track in an old television sitcom.

"Take ten," he called as he shut down his camera, unwilling to waste any more film when Jackie was obviously having an off day. He laid his light meter on a clean tarp spread over the pine needles, then walked over to where she stood, her bare toes tracing patterns in the deep pine needles covering the forest floor. "All right, Jane. What gives?"

She bit her lip in an uncharacteristic nervous movement. Greg had thought all day she'd been simply annoyed with him since yesterday's meeting, but now he caught a glimpse of worry in her green gaze.

"I think I've lost my voice." She let go of her vine and turned to face him, hands on barely covered hips.

Greg forced himself to concentrate on her words and not those perfect curves. "Impossible. Your voice sounds dynamite. You're just not projecting."

She shook her head. "You don't understand. I wanted to do a really good job today so we could put this shoot behind us. But no matter how hard I try, I can't seem to tap into my vocal energy and I'm afraid I've done something to screw up my voice and my confidence."

He was at a total loss too because he could never

seem to focus around a half-naked Jackie. During his production days, he'd filmed women in bikinis hundreds of times and never batted an eyelash.

Okay, maybe an occasional eyelash. But it sure as hell had never robbed him of all ability to think or comprehend.

He pulled her denim jacket out of the opened back of the location van and tucked the coat around her shoulders. "There. Care to run that by me one more time? Your voice is giving you trouble?"

She slid her arms into the sleeves of her jacket and scowled. "No. Actually I've been giving my voice trouble lately and I think it's taking revenge on me today."

Still her words refused to penetrate his brain. He pulled her over to the van so they could sit on the carpeted floor just inside the opened doors.

"I'm slow today, I know. You want to explain how you can give your voice trouble?" Preferably the sooner the better so they could get out of here before he lost his ability to maintain professional distance. He'd wanted an opportunity to see her again, to convince her maybe they had a shot at making something work between them, but not if he had to resort to sensual manipulation to get what he wanted.

He'd at least wait until they weren't working to try those means of persuasion. He reached into the cooler resting behind the fender for the back left wheel and pulled out two drinks. While he flipped open the top of his bottle of water, he passed her a chilled drink of her own.

Jackie took the bottle gratefully, allowing the cold to

seep into her palm in the vain hope it might settle her jumpy nerves. She stared out into the forest of dense trees and sighed.

How could she explain about her voice? She definitely had not wanted to discuss this with Greg, but despite her best efforts, her pipes were falling flat today.

Whether the problem was real or imagined, it was causing her to mess up take after take. She couldn't see any choice but to explain the whole problem.

"I tried to manipulate my voice," she ventured, not daring to make eye contact during an explanation Greg would no doubt find ridiculous. "Have you ever heard the stage wisdom that you can't truly sing until you've screwed?"

Greg nearly choked on his Perrier.

Wide-eyed, he stared at her while he coughed.

Jackie thumped him on the back and scrambled to explain. Since when had she been known for tact?

"That sounds incredibly crass, I know. A music teacher explained it to me that way once and I guess the phrasing stuck. But you get the drift, right?"

Greg only coughed harder.

"My teacher just meant that—"

Greg held up one hand in the international stop symbol. "I get it," he rasped.

"Good." She nodded, pleased to have at least laid the groundwork for the rest of this inane discussion. Sure, it might be a little embarrassing to talk this over with Greg, but if she didn't clear the air about what she'd done, her guilty conscience might never allow her to sing again.

"I had that old adage in my mind when you and I first met, I suppose. And part of me really wanted to know if it was true. So in a way I guess I used our relationship to—"

"Wait a minute." Greg took a few last coughs and then sat up straight again. "You're telling me you thought about this when we first met? Like even that first night at Mike's bachelor party?"

She was powerless to deny it. "I know it was underhanded and all, but—"

"So in other words, you were already thinking of me in *that* way from day one."

Did that make her the world's most wanton woman? "I guess so."

Greg smiled. Big. "Do you honestly think I'd mind if you were maneuvering ways to get me into bed from the moment we met?"

She frowned. "I'd hardly say that was the case."

"Damn." He took a swig from his water bottle and set it aside. "I was starting to enjoy being a sex object."

"You're making it very difficult for me to absolve myself."

"Is there some grave sin in here I'm missing?"

"I'm afraid I sort of used our relationship as a way to find out if the old adage was true, but now I can't even have the satisfaction of a newly passionate voice because I've been too guilty to exercise the gift ever since we, well, you know." How incredibly awkward. Jackie had never been adept at intimate conversations, preferring to hide her feelings behind a smile and a song.

Greg scratched his jaw as his gaze followed a yellow

butterfly flitting around a small patch of flowers. "And you think by confessing this to me you'll win your voice back?"

"It's the only other thing I can think of to do. I've tried herbal tea and hot showers and—"

"You're going about this all wrong." He plucked her bottle of water from her hand and set it aside. "It's obvious to me that our first sexual encounter didn't work for you for some reason. You were left with a worse voice than you had to begin with. The only solution is for us to try again."

She blinked. "You're suggesting more sex will solve the problem?"

Slowly, he nodded, not quite managing to keep the wicked sparkle from his dark eyes. "Your creative abilities are important to the shoot, Jackie. I'm willing to take one for the team if it means you'll recover your voice."

"How noble of you." A smile tugged at her lips. She couldn't help but appreciate a man who could make her feel so at ease with herself after such an uncomfortable moment. Damned if that De Costa charm wasn't melting her limited defenses. "Bet you were quite a smooth talker with the girls back in high school, weren't you?"

He straightened his tie. "Where do you think I honed my negotiating skills?"

Greg reached for her, sliding his fingers down an escaped strand of her hair. Shivery sensation tripped through her scalp and down the back of her neck.

"You prepared for network television by talking

girls out of their sweaters?" Her voice hit a low, husky range she usually reserved for torch songs.

"I was a kid from the Southside, Jackie. I took my lessons wherever I could find them."

She knew he was still teasing her, still plying her with the De Costa charm that had won her that first night in an overcrowded bar full of bachelors. Yet she heard the hint of pride in his voice, the tiny thread of defensiveness even.

Greg had played piano in a bar to work his way through college while Jackie's parents couldn't enroll her in enough world-renowned programs to nurture her musical gifts. For the first time, she caught a glimpse of why Greg might have traded the production work he loved for a penthouse position with big visibility.

Maybe that Southside youth was still looking for affirmation. And maybe, just now, she wanted more than anything to be the woman to provide it. If only for a few hours.

Their first time had been all about her—what she wanted and what she'd fantasized about. Maybe Greg deserved to know that a woman could give him something too, without expecting anything in return.

"How about superstitious singers with big dreams and even bigger hang-ups?" She allowed herself to touch him, to trace the line of his suspender over the taut muscle of his chest. "Do you still take those wherever you can find them?"

"Actually, I only take one of those." His fingers skimmed the column of her neck down to the hollow at the base of her throat. "And then only when she's amenable."

Her heart slammed a heavy backbeat to his light touch.

She was feeling far too amenable right now. She wanted nothing so much as to close her eyes and absorb the feel of Greg's caress, to stretch out underneath him and—

But was she making a huge mistake? Rationalizing what she wanted because she wanted it so very badly? Falling for a man whose lifestyle choices contrasted with hers at every turn could only lead to heartache.

Amazing sex, maybe, but definitely heartache in the end.

His hand strayed lower, edging open her denim jacket to sketch a tingly path toward her breast. She fought the urge to arch her back and plaster herself to the pleasure of those questing fingers.

Desperate to squelch the need spiraling through her, Jackie searched her mind for a distracting conversational thread. If she could start a discussion about the jingle, maybe she could dodge the heat building between them.

Of course, thinking of the jingle only made her think of her voice, which in turn only made her think of sex.

But opening her mouth to speak, to utter any words that might help her regain her sanity, Jackie found herself saying, "I wonder if we'll get paid overtime if we take a few hours to really explore this 'follow your natural instincts' concept?"

She'd worry about the fallout later. Right now she could only think, breathe, and touch Greg.

He ran a finger up the suede lacing of her bikini halter-top and pulled the skinny strap to untie the knot that held it in place. The buttery-smooth straps slithered down her collarbone and released the straining cups, freeing her breasts beneath her unfastened jacket.

"Probably not." He spread her jacket open wide and inched the denim down her shoulders. "But I'd gladly work around the clock the next few days to make up the time if I can have those hours right now. Right here."

The spring sun warmed her skin. Greg's hot gaze only made her temperature soar all the more, made her cheeks heat with awareness.

What made this wild, wide-open space suddenly seem even more intimate than the steamy confines of a tiny sound studio?

Greg tipped her chin up, forced her to meet his intent stare. "Are you sure you're okay with this, Jackie?"

Ever the gentleman, chivalrous Greg was giving her an out.

The man could wrap her in a tablecloth when she lost her costume. He could spirit her away from a bachelor party full of wolf whistles. And he could smooth an awkward afternoon with her super-intimidating parents by sheer force of his magnetic charm.

He'd saved her from herself more than once, but today wasn't a day she cared to be saved.

In fact, right now she could only think about how

good it would feel to throw herself directly into the fire that was Greg De Costa.

"I thought we decided to quit being noble today." She inserted a finger into the intricate knot of his tie and tugged. "You don't have to ask me if I'm sure I know what I'm doing here, and I don't have to feel guilty about wrapping my legs around you and locking our bodies together until my voice hits opera diva status. Got it?"

She untwined the knot and slid the tie back and forth around his neck like a shoeshine cloth. The soft hiss of silk caressing crisp cotton was a sound a woman could grow accustomed to, a sound that triggered hormones flowing, mouth watering and sexual adrenaline pumping.

"Understood. In fact, I've never felt less noble in all my life." No sooner had he said the words than he scooped her out of the van and carried her across the makeshift set.

Her heart jumped to be in his arms, her temple nestled next to an impressive bicep encased in white cotton.

She couldn't suppress an irreverent giggle.

"You Tarzan, me Jane?" she asked as he settled her on the clean tarp where he kept his extra camera equipment. He laid her down on her back, carefully fanning out her hair alongside her.

"That's it exactly." He cleared aside the lenses with the sweep of his arm before he stretched out beside her under the canopy of green leaves.

Picking up a broad maple leaf from the tarp, he

teased the ruffled edges along the bare skin of her belly, then skimmed it along the edge of her suede bikini bottoms.

He leaned over her to enter her line of vision. "And as long as you remember who's lord of the jungle today, I'll remember to treat you like my queen."

"Is that so?" Curiosity skipped through her. Jackie had limited sensual experience before Greg, but she was quite certain she'd never been given the royal treatment in bed.

She rather hoped it entailed the scandalous act she currently imagined.

"That's a promise." Greg tugged at the rawhide straps holding her string bikini bottom to her hips. "If I had known the other night was your first time, I never would have dreamed up the against-the-door scenario."

Her legs trembled as he drew the untied strap over her hipbone and around the front of her belly, lower and lower. Heat swirled at the juncture of her thighs.

"Don't knock the against-the-door position," she managed between the little gasps he wrung from her with his teasing seduction. "I'm thinking it might turn out to be one of my all-time favorites."

He bent over her to kiss her navel, then fanned a warm breath against the barely hanging on bottoms of her Jane outfit.

Shifting his body lower on the tarp, he positioned himself over her thighs.

"Why don't you close your eyes and reserve judgment on that until after I've given you a taste...of heaven?"

13

GREG WAS FIVE SECONDS away from fulfilling every fantasy he'd ever had about Jackie in her Jane outfit.

She lay warm and welcoming beneath him, her green eyes dark as the shady forest around them. The citrusy scent of her perfume filled his nostrils, the light notes growing stronger in direct response to the rising heat of her arousal.

Greg had probably scratched a thousand dollars worth of camera lenses in his haste to clear a place for them to stretch out, but he didn't care. Something about Jackie made him wild, made him seriously consider ditching all his career concerns to follow his passions.

All that mattered to him right now was giving Jackie the slow, pull-out-all-the-stops experience their frenzied, high-heat encounter in the sound studio hadn't provided.

Their gazes connected for a long moment, and then slowly, Jackie's eyes closed.

Just like he'd asked.

With that small gesture, she had given her unspoken permission for him to touch, taste and tease her into sensual oblivion.

He'd been rock-hard before she'd given that tacit approval. Still, a new wave of blood surged south at her provocative consent, hot and thick. This woman had a way of rendering him practically light-headed.

His only hope for surviving the next round of slow torment was to close his eyes too, shutting out the erotic picture of Jackie naked and flushed beneath him, her nipples taut pink peaks.

He didn't need to see to know where to place his next kiss. His mouth found the soft flesh of her inner thigh and she gasped, arched.

The sun shone warm on his back through the trees, reminding him to unbutton his shirt, to tug apart the last strap holding Jackie's suit together. Her fingers moved restlessly with his as he untied the rawhide knot, her half-frantic fingers only slowing him down.

His own need for her cranked up another notch, making him desperate to unveil the last part of her that remained covered. He pulled Jackie's impatient hands away from the ties and imprisoned her wrists lightly at her sides.

Never one to take direction well off the set, she arched her hips, pushing him right over the last thread of his own restraints.

He released her wrists to cup the suede scrap of material in his hand, cupping the warm heat of her along with it. Jackie moaned, sighed, writhed beneath him, her fingers dancing over his shoulders in helpless agitation, her short nails lightly scratching him every now and then.

Not that he cared.

Those light scores distracted him just enough to keep

from losing his mind and plunging himself deep inside her. Her heat, her scent, permeated the damp, buttery suede until he thought he'd lose his mind if he couldn't taste her.

Only then did he allow himself to peel the material down her slender thighs and kiss her more intimately than ever before.

She tasted so sweet he didn't know how long he could last. He gripped her thighs with both hands, trying to anchor himself against the sultry rush of sensation threatening to thwart his best effort to take Jackie higher than she'd ever been.

He welcomed the increased urgency of her fingers as she gripped his shoulders, clung to him and cried out. That slight bite of her nails kept his hunger for her at bay just long enough for him to tease the hot center of her, to draw her more deeply into his mouth and—

She flew apart in a series of shockwaves Greg felt clear to his toes. Her fingers knotted in his hair as she shouted out a primitive cry worthy of the queen of the jungle.

Greg sensed more than saw the scattering of birds into the trees at her ear-splitting call. He could only cradle her to him as the last of the aftershocks wore away, warding off the fierce need to possess her, the sudden archaic desire to make her his for today, tomorrow and forever after.

It seemed once again he didn't need to be noble, however.

As the roaring of his blood in his ears quieted just a little, he became aware of Jackie's whispered command. "Please. Please. Please." She repeated the word over and over, tugging on his shoulder as if she could raise him up from his perch between her thighs.

Right then he vowed to make something work between them. He would convince her somehow, someway that they needed to be together, because no woman had ever suited him so perfectly as this wild woman, his insatiable jungle queen who'd saved herself just for him.

LITTLE TREMORS STILL danced through her, her insides quivering with the most amazing combination of complete satisfaction and residual hunger to have all of Greg inside of her.

Right now.

She'd never experienced anything as earth rocking and toe curling as those electric moments when he had catapulted her beyond the green forest and straight to the stars. But still, even that amazing pleasure wasn't quite enough to fulfill her. She needed everything he had to offer her.

With impatient hands, she clutched at his shoulders until he obeyed her wordless command to position himself above her. She stared up at the flexing of sinewy shoulders as he walked his arms up the sides of her until he bracketed her body with his hands.

She wanted to mold, to touch, to absorb every inch of tanned muscle, but there wasn't time. Not when her body hungered for his with a sharp ache that wouldn't be denied.

Her fingers dove for his trousers, unfastening, unbuttoning and unzipping anything in the way of what she wanted.

Greg rolled away from her just long enough to slide off his pants, his boxers, all the clothes she'd been fumbling with. In two seconds flat he was naked.

And very, very ready.

Jackie couldn't seem to tear her gaze away from all that...maleness.

"Second thoughts?" his voice whispered over her, humor threading through the words.

"No." She reached for him, tentatively stroking the rigid flesh. His breath hissed, caught, held, drawing her attention up to his face.

His eyes closed, his jaw muscle flexing as tightly as the rest of him.

She marveled that her touch could wield so much power. "It's just that I didn't get to really see you the other night. At least not like this."

Her fingers glided over the expanse of smooth skin, fascinated that he could fit inside her. She might have continued her exploration if Greg hadn't gripped her wrist and stilled her hand.

"I'm teetering on the edge, Jackie." His dark eyes glittered with a fierce light.

"You're not going over without me." She straddled his thighs while he reached for the protection he must have fished out of his wallet when he removed his pants. "I'm wresting every ounce of pleasure I can from this day."

If she couldn't have Greg long-term, she could at

least give herself the gift of a perfect day, the memory of phenomenal sex.

Only, this charged encounter didn't feel so much like simply sex. There was a deeper intimacy involved than in their sizzling night at the sound studio.

Before she could question the matter any further, Greg's hands slid around her hips, lifting her up to position her, to fit her perfectly to him.

And then thought became impossible. As soon as the hard length of him touched that most sensitive part of her, she was lost. She closed her eyes, focusing on the sensation of him entering her, filling her.

Fulfilling her.

He allowed her to find a rhythm, to direct their movements around the tarp under the warm spring sun. And she was obviously communing with her inner Jane. Something about the absolute freedom of being outside, of being naked in nature and still having a man find her desirable, made her feel wild.

She could have found her peak, could have easily moved into another state of bliss because she was in control on top of him. Yet each time she moved closer to that heart-stopping goal, Greg's hands steadied her hips, refused to let her go there yet.

Each time she rebuilt the sensual momentum, the delicious heat between her thighs, the peak loomed all the higher and therefore, all the more enticing.

The third time, she pried her eyes open, wondering how the man could possess such self-control. His gaze was on her from the moment she forced her lids apart.

Obviously, he'd been watching her all along, perhaps gauging her arousal by her expression.

That he watched her didn't come close to embarrassing her. Rather, his intense stare reflected only dark tenderness, an emotional depth that left her feeling far more exposed than the loss of her suede bikini.

"Jackie." He cupped her face in his hand, cradling her cheek with the broad expanse of his palm. Her head tilted into that warm strength, as if she could melt right into his touch.

With a low growl, Greg rolled them sideways until they'd reversed positions. He lowered his mouth to hers, steadying her mouth with one hand.

Gently, he merged their mouths, fused their bodies, and began the slow climb to the peak he'd been denying her.

Heat swirled through her, lush desire fluttered low in her belly. She wanted this, wanted him, more than she could remember wanting anything in her life.

The scent of his musky aftershave mingled with the green scents of pine and grass. She reached up to drape her arms around his neck, to hold on for dear life as the force of that peak built, threatened, and then flooded over her like a tidal wave.

She cried out her satisfaction with a voice only the lord of the jungle could appreciate. Sound emanated from her toes until it launched from her lips with enough projection to be heard two counties away.

Still, she could have yodeled from coast to coast and not quite have voiced everything she felt in that heated moment. The force of her emotions, the sudden overwhelming possessiveness for the man inside her, scared her.

As he drew her into his arms, she couldn't help but think she ought to slip on her Nike high-tops and start running—fast and furious—before she lost more of her heart than she'd ever be able to retrieve.

She'd thought she could show him that a woman could be giving. That she could give him something beautiful and not expect anything in return, unlike the women of his past.

But she'd ended up giving him far, far too much.

As the last little waves of pleasure rolled through her, clearing her mind for rational thought to return, Jackie knew there was only one thing left to give him. As much as it was tearing her up inside, she knew she needed to put someone else's needs before her own for a change. Before if she failed in life, she would only hurt herself.

But hurting Greg was unacceptable. Unconscionable.

So she would grant him the only thing she could that was guaranteed not to disappoint him somewhere down the road.

His freedom.

GREG WRAPPED HIS ARMS more tightly around Jackie's waist, fully intending to make the most of every minute they had together before they needed to return to filming. Her heart thumped a steady pulse against his chest, the soft drumming as reassuring as a tried and true rhythm track behind adventurous vocals.

He didn't fully comprehend why this unconventional woman seemed to anchor him, but she did. When he was with her, he didn't feel the need to scramble up to the next level of success, didn't feel obligated to continually prove himself.

The sun dipped in and out of wispy clouds high above, causing dappled shadows to dance over their bodies under the leafy green canopy. A chill danced through Jackie, her answering shiver urging Greg to pull one edge of the tarp over her shoulder.

Jackie sat up first, sliding away from him when all he wanted to do was hold her and figure out what in the hell had just happened between them.

No way had the past hour been about sex.

Greg had indulged in plenty of sex in his lifetime and none of it had ever compelled him to wrap up the woman in question and take her home with him. Forever.

The sun shifted again, sending spears of light over Jackie as she moved silently toward the van where she retrieved her Jane garb. He watched her slide into the buff-colored suede, her dancer's body haloed by the midday sun—and he knew.

He had fallen in love with Zing-O-Gram girl.

The sexy feline in high-tops.

The wild and uninhibited Jane.

But most of all, he had fallen in love with Jackie Brady, the talented singer and composer who wasn't afraid to cause a scene and who probably knew as much about the Red Sox as he did.

The revelation would have been cause for celebration if the woman in question didn't look ready to flee.

Somehow, during Greg's lightbulb moment, she had dressed, reassembled her queen of the jungle hair, and was already making strides toward her tree.

"Shouldn't we try to get this wrapped before the sun sets?" she called over one shoulder, positioning the vine so she'd be ready to jump.

Greg scrambled to his feet.

"Wait a minute." He definitely wasn't in a position to make a big declaration. A man claiming to be in love ought to at least have on a pair of pants. "We need to talk."

She frowned. "Maybe we ought to wait to talk on the ride home. We'll be even further behind if we lose the sunlight—"

"Screw the sunlight." He edged into his trousers, stuffed his bare toes back into his shoes, and inserted himself between Jackie and the tree.

"What I have to say to you is too important to wait." He'd never been one to hesitate in going after what he wanted and he wasn't about to put this off either. He reached for her, cradling her face in his hands.

"But—"

He shushed any objections with a finger pressed to her lips.

"I love you, Jackie."

Even the birds in the background seemed to go silent in the wake of his declaration. Jackie stared up at him with wide-green eyes, her expression resembling more mild horror than overjoyed.

He pulled her back toward the van, back toward the safety of that denim jacket he'd pulled off her earlier.

"I know it sounds crazy because we haven't even known each other that long." He picked up the jacket from the floor of the location vehicle and slid it around her shoulders.

She clutched the lapels to her chest like a woman in shock. Still, she tilted her gaze up to his, her voice hoarse with some emotion he couldn't name.

"It *is* crazy."

He shook his head, more certain of this than anything he'd ever experienced. "It's true. And I know it's true because I'm laying myself on the line here for you, Jackie. A risk I've never taken with any other woman in my whole life."

A single tear leaked from the corner of her eye.

With a looming fear that he'd already screwed up this round of negotiations, Greg had the impression it wasn't a happy tear.

He waded in deeper, determined to have it all out today, to show her everything in his heart and win her over for good.

"Let's negotiate here. *I* want you, Jackie, and I'm in love with you. That means I want to be with you tomorrow, and the day after that, and the day after that." He tucked a stray strand of cinnamon hair behind her ear, willing her to see what a good thing this could be. "What do *you* want?"

Another tear slid free, even though Greg could swear he spied a hint of yearning in her eyes.

"I want to be the right woman for you, but I'm not."
The resolution in her eyes gave him a moment's pause.

"Why don't I get to be the one to decide that?"

"Because maybe your decision making isn't reliable right now. What if you're only reacting to the phenomenal sex?"

He damn well knew his own mind. But he had the feeling that wouldn't hold much weight with Jackie right now.

Jackie sniffled, swiping away her tears with the back of her hand. "Besides, remember what you said you wanted? Something about us being together tomorrow and the day after and the day after. Yet you would be embarrassed of me the day after *that*." She met his gaze head on, with a frankness that told him she meant every word. "You couldn't deny as much just a few days ago."

"That's because I was still thinking with my damn head in the sand and putting my career before me. But I'm not going to do that anymore. Haven't I achieved enough in this business where I don't need to worry about my professional image all the time? What's the point of working your ass off if it doesn't buy you the freedom to be who and what you really want to be?" The more he talked, the more sense the whole thing made to him.

But he seemed to be the only one buying it.

Jackie tugged his hands from her cheeks and held them in her own. She took a small but definite step back, as if she could retreat from him and what he wanted from her.

"You don't understand. Even if you never want to move up in your career, that doesn't take away the fact that you already have a huge, high-visibility position that demands a fair amount of social kowtowing. First of all, I am not a banquet-and-ceremony kind of girl. I don't mingle well, yet I don't play a wallflower very well. Sooner or later, I will show up with whiskers on for some important function or another and it will be all over between us. You'll be disappointed, and I'll be heartbroken. Sorry, not interested." She spun on her heel, her determined strides taking her back to her tree.

Greg followed, winging her around by the elbow before she could scale the branches. "But I told you, my work is not going to take precedence over my life anymore. A man is entitled to reprioritize, damn it, and I want you at the top of the list."

Jackie closed her eyes for a long moment. Greg was afraid more tears might follow, but instead of a waterfall, he found only fire in her green gaze.

"But no matter how much you tell me work is not more important to you, I have a difficult time believing it when your love for me isn't declared so much as it's negotiated, or when you attempt to convince me of your new nonbusiness focus with talk of reprioritization and list making. Are we going to consolidate too?" She took off her jacket and thrust it at him. "I'm sorry, Greg, but those are just words. The fact that they also happen to be the words of corporate America just reinforces my opinion all the more. You're devoted to your job and a woman like me will only get in the way of what you want."

Greg took her jacket, folding it carefully under one arm. She might as well have just handed his damn heart back to him too. She couldn't have made her stance any clearer.

And that hurt a hell of a lot more than he ever would have anticipated.

Still, he saw a tiny loophole in her tough-as-nails position. And if he was drawing on his experience as a crack contract negotiator to see as much, he didn't give a rat's ass. He would pull out all the stops to give her what she wanted.

To win what he wanted more than anything.

She thought his declaration of love was the result of great sex? Then he'd romance her when there wasn't a bed, or an office chair, or a clean tarp in sight.

She thought his career meant more to him than she did?

Then he'd show her evidence to the contrary.

All he had to come up with was visible, concrete proof.

14

JACKIE SPRAWLED OUT ON her picnic table in the backyard of her brownstone Saturday morning, the day of her cancelled twenty-fifth birthday party. She was too upset to party anyway.

She rested her chin on one hand while she wrote the finishing touches for her dancing hippo operetta—a triumphant finale in which the main character follows her dreams no matter how bizarre or downright laughable they seem to the rest of the world.

At least Jackie hoped the ending was triumphant.

Everything else she'd written in the days following her confrontation with Greg had been rather dark and emotional. She'd penned enough public service music to draw attention to teen runaways, domestic violence and hospice care services this week to make her wonder if she could ever compose something upbeat again.

But she was being creative. Maybe more creative than she'd ever been in her life.

Whoever had first said you couldn't sing until you'd screwed had grossly oversimplified the case. A more accurate adage should say something like you couldn't fully tap into your creative energies until you've experienced the kind of wretched, all-consuming heartache that comes with intimacy.

As a jingle writer, Jackie could certainly see where the former was quite a bit catchier.

As a woman, she couldn't quite get past the heartache part.

Happy birthday to me.

She and Greg had wrapped their commercial in record time, only requiring that first day on location. Jackie had recorded a new vocals track in the wild, too, but Greg had insisted he didn't need her help editing the whole thing together. He'd dropped her off at the studio late that night with a polite kiss on the cheek that had felt like a permanent goodbye, but other than that, she hadn't seen or heard from him in days.

By now, she had turned their fateful conversation inside out to see if she'd been too quick to walk away from a good thing, but she still kept returning to the same conclusion. A man so tied to his work—and in turn, public opinion—would only regret a relationship with someone like her in the long run.

Not that being right gave her any great sense of satisfaction as she ate her way through every comfort food she could think of, churned out angst-filled, emotional jingles, and tried to think up good excuses for skipping today's unveiling party at Shamus's estate.

She couldn't face Greg again. Not yet.

As she racked her brain for an appropriate excuse, something more inventive than laryngitis, Jackie heard a feminine voice drift her way from the front of the brownstone.

"Yoo-hoo! Jackie?"

No one said yoo-hoo but a kindergarten teacher.

Jackie closed her notebook and turned off the beat track she'd been running to help her finish the musical composition.

"I'm back here, Hannah," she called, hopping off the picnic table to greet the friend she hadn't seen all week. They'd spoken on the phone a couple of times, enough that Hannah knew Greg and Jackie had broken up, but Jackie hadn't mentioned the party or her birthday to her.

As she rounded the corner of the building she nearly plowed right into Hannah, who had ditched her blond braids in favor of two tiny gold barrettes bearing the likeness of Minnie Mouse. Dressed in a tea-length floral sundress, she looked downright elegant.

"What gives?" Jackie asked, flicking one of her friend's diaphanous cap sleeves. "You doing a bridesmaid luncheon or something?"

Hannah rolled her eyes. "Hello? I'm going to the commercial unveiling. Why aren't you dressed yet?"

Panic zinged through Jackie.

"You're going?" How did Hannah even know about the commercial unveiling?

"Greg invited Mike and me. Mike's riding to the party with Greg because they went early to help set up this morning. I thought I'd see if you wanted to go with me."

"I don't think I feel well." Jackie coughed. "I think I'm coming down with laryngitis." She rasped out the last few words for good measure.

Hannah looped her arm through Jackie's and towed her toward the brownstone.

"Nice try. If I have to go to a party with Mike when we *still* haven't ironed out whether or not we'll be getting married next weekend, you can damn well face Greg for a couple of hours."

JACKIE THOUGHT SHE'D BEEN transported to Newport once she got a look at Shamus's north Boston spread. The sprawling brick facade looked big enough to be a dorm at Harvard rather than a single-family residence. The yard alone rivaled the size of a couple of football fields.

"Are you sure we have the right address?" Jackie asked, wondering if she should have worn something more formal than the navy-and-white polka dot dress Hannah had coerced her into. "This looks a bit upscale for me."

For that matter, this kind of highbrow party was precisely the reason she and Greg would never make a good couple. Greg could sip champagne and make small talk all day with anyone. Jackie would rather be the entertainment for this crowd than to have to blend in.

"A house is a house. Don't let it scare you." Hannah adjusted her barrettes and smoothed her skirt. "Besides, Mike told me this Shamus guy is really down to earth."

True enough.

Surely she could handle blending in for one afternoon out of her whole life, right? She just wished she didn't need to juggle that task with having to face

Greg, too. Angsty, heartbroken women didn't tend to blend well anywhere.

They were only a few steps from the car when Chip, Greg's administrative assistant from WBCI pulled up in a golf cart to offer them a ride.

"The party is in the backyard, ladies, and I'm your official shuttle. Hop in." He jogged around the cart in his seersucker shirt and blue suspenders imprinted with tiny tennis rackets to open the door for them.

She and Hannah slid inside the cart and held on for the ride across the massive lawns.

Jackie's nerves frayed a little more with every bounce and sway of the vehicle. Her socializing skills ranged from poor to nonexistent. How could she fake her way through the whole afternoon?

To distract herself, she tried to fish more information out of Hannah about how things stood between her and Mike.

"So you never explained why you and Mike haven't finished finalizing your plans," she prodded, craning her neck to see any signs of a party as they curved around to the side of the monstrous house.

Hannah sighed. "I sort of feel like it's his responsibility to get everything back on track if he wants to go through with it. I planned the whole thing to start with, and then after I made my stand about wanting to see a few sparks fly, I guess I hoped Mike would take that a step further and really commit himself to the wedding."

She fiddled with the hem of her floral dress and shrugged. "I haven't said a word about it since we tentatively made up, so I don't have a clue if I'll be walking down the aisle next Saturday or not. One thing is certain, though. If Mike doesn't initiate a discussion about it soon, I'm not even getting out of bed next weekend."

And then there would be *two* De Costa men back in circulation. Beware, women of Boston. Devastating charm on the loose.

"He'll say something," Jackie assured her. Hadn't Greg told her once that he and Mike differed in how they approached life? Greg put all his efforts into his career while Mike seemed to put his efforts into enjoying life. A man like that wouldn't let go of the woman he loved.

Unlike his brother.

Finally the Back To Nature screening party came into view—a milling group of at least a hundred people scattered around an organically shaped pool and landscaped grounds leading down to an intercoastal waterway. The well-heeled gathering resembled a garden party cocktail hour more than any business celebration, but apparently if the client had deep pockets and was holding the party at his home, it could be as lavish as he wanted.

The Back To Nature theme had translated to an outdoor haven, sort of *Blue Lagoon* meets Nantucket. A bar constructed of bamboo sat at one end of the party, while a low stage decorated in ivy and grapevine dominated the center. Men in seersucker suits and women in wide-brimmed hats peopled the scene. Friends of

Shamus's perhaps, as Jackie didn't recognize anyone she knew.

Until two figures garbed in black separated from the crowd to approach the golf cart.

"Darling!" Niall Brady called, his black floral tie the only nod to the garden party theme in his otherwise austere garb. He always dressed as if he could take the stage at Carnegie Hall at any moment and all he'd need is to don a bow tie.

"Jacquelyn!" Deirdre Breslin Brady, wearing a straw hat with a broad black ribbon, echoed a split second later.

Jackie's parents converged on them. What on earth were they doing here, at Shamus's commercial unveiling party?

Before she could ask—

"Happy Birthday to you," Niall began, Deirdre chiming in a stanza later so that they sang the traditional song as a round.

Jackie had to smile at the small nod to her eccentric preferences. Perhaps her parents were beginning to accept her for who she was and not just who they wanted her to be.

"Thank you." She hugged them both, making a special effort not to crush her mother's linen suit. After introducing Hannah to them both, she couldn't help but comment on their unexpected presence. "I'm surprised to see you here."

"Shortly after you called to let us know you couldn't attend the birthday party, Gregory called to invite us to the commercial screening," her father explained, as he accepted a glass of champagne from a tuxedoed waiter. "We wanted to be here for your big moment."

Greg had invited her parents? The people he knew darn well she danced around whenever and wherever she could?

"He said you wrote the music for the piece?" Deirdre asked.

"It's a commercial jingle, Mom." No sense getting their hopes up she'd penned the next 1812 Overture or anything.

"Gregory says it has a lot of edgy appeal," her father corrected her. "Debussy was very edgy in his day, too. And look where he is in the musical canon."

Jackie tried very hard not to roll her eyes as she wondered if she had Greg to thank for the comparison.

"Perhaps I had better find Greg and thank him." Jackie smiled, extricating herself and Hannah with what she hoped was semi-politeness to scope the party terrain for the man she was now quite ready to confront.

"I can't believe he not only invited my parents without telling me, but he also got their hopes up that I was going to wow them with some display of musical genius." How could he when he knew she'd had professional insecurities in light of her prodigy heritage?

Hannah frowned. "Maybe he's just proud of you."

Maybe. But he had to know her highbrow parents wouldn't be hugely impressed by her somewhat suggestive lyrics urging a back to nature approach to life.

She peered around an ice sculpture of a palm tree for signs of Greg.

No luck there.

But another De Costa male appeared in her line of sight. Dressed in a steely-gray suit that looked tailor-made to his broad shoulders and carrying a bouquet of daisies a woman who wore Minnie Mouse barrettes would surely appreciate, Mike strode toward them.

Jackie could feel the nervous energy and downright excitement practically radiating from Hannah.

"Oh my God," her friend whispered, sliding a hand over her silky blond hair. "Is he not a to-die-for male?"

"So you're pretty sure those sparks you wanted are all present and accounted for?" Jackie teased, ruthlessly squashing a tiny flare of envy for Hannah. Why couldn't she and Greg have reached the kind of accord Mike and Hannah had?

"They're so accounted for, I may combust with them," Hannah shot back a split second before she launched herself in his path, laying an enthusiastic smooch on him until her barrette slid sideways. Somehow, they had learned to compromise enough so that Mike reserved his charm for Hannah alone, and Hannah had obviously found plenty of new ways to engage his attention.

Jackie could practically hear the wedding bells in the background as Mike spirited Hannah away to a quiet table near the far end of the pool.

Leaving her just a little forlorn in the crowd of people she didn't know.

"Ms. Brady?" a masculine voice hailed her through the crowd.

Turning, she found seersucker and freckles.

"Hi, Chip. Have you moved on from the shuttling job?" She snagged a crab-smothered cracker from a passing tray and hoped maybe Chip would shoot the breeze with her for a few minutes before she had to—gasp—mingle.

He grinned, the tips of his ears turning an interesting shade of pink. "Actually, I've moved into setting up for the day's entertainment. Mr. De Costa wanted me to be sure you had a front-row view."

GREG STARED THROUGH THE cabana window at Chip blushing wildly while he talked to Jackie.

The woman had a knack for distracting the most driven of men.

He silently applauded Chip's maneuvering, however, as his administrative assistant escorted Jackie to the exact spot Greg had wanted her to stand. He was putting on this cockamamie display for her benefit alone, so he would be sure she didn't miss a moment of his first public performance since his college days playing piano in the bar.

The door of the cabana opened to reveal his brother.

"How you holding together in here? You getting cold feet?" Mike edged his way into the simply furnished area, maneuvering between two striped loungers draped in extra beach towels.

"Not a chance."

Mike grinned as he poked his brother's bared bicep. "You sure you're not going to make her swoon with all this flesh you're flaunting?"

Greg flicked the daisy in Mike's lapel.

"Watch it, Romeo. Don't you have a woman of your own you're supposed to be courting right now?" Greg snagged a bottle of top-shelf champagne from the caterer's stash in the cabana kitchen. Wrestling it open, he took a page from Mike's book and sipped straight from the bottle as if it were a longneck.

Sometimes the unconventional approach could be downright freeing.

"I'll have you know I'm being a very attentive date. I mentioned a few ideas for the wedding next weekend, and Hannah went into total sex kitten mode. If I'd have known talking flowers and organists would have her groping my organ, I would done it a long time ago." He picked at the buttons of his jacket cuff. "Hell, if I'd have known how much losing her would hurt, I would have done anything long ago."

He let go of the button and shrugged. "She's chatting it up with someone she knew from college, so I am on the official mission to the punch bowl." Mike nudged Greg's arm. "You gonna share any of that stuff or are you going to make me drink the damn punch?"

"I thought you didn't consume any beverage with bubbles." Greg cradled the champagne protectively with both hands, happy for Mike that he and Hannah had worked through their differences.

Much to their mutual satisfaction, it seemed.

Would he and Jackie be that lucky? Or would she run screaming in the other direction when she got an eyeful of his upcoming performance?

Mike snorted. "The bubbly drink is seeming downright manly next to punch. Fork it over, bro, or I'll send you out into the crowd of partygoers in nothing but a loincloth." He stared meaningfully at Greg's costume of choice. "Oh wait. You're already going to do that."

Greg couldn't help but cringe as he stared down the length of his bare chest to the tan suede material tied around his waist.

Now he knew how Jackie felt having to traipse around as Jane all week. His Tarzan garb left a lot to be desired.

"You're walking on thin ice if you're expecting a best man to show up at your wedding next weekend." Greg passed the champagne and checked out the window to see how the entertainment preparations were shaping up. "Looks like Hannah's saying goodbye to that friend of hers."

"Damn. I didn't even find the punch bowl yet." Mike shoved the bottle back into Greg's arms and wiped the bubbles with the sleeve of his suit. "You sure you want to go through with this? Even if it costs you the career you've worked your ass off to achieve?"

Greg didn't even hesitate. "Didn't you tell me once that not every woman cares about burning ambition? I'm thinking about going back into production anyway."

"You realize you're taking romantic advice from the guy who nearly lost his bride on the way to the altar, right?"

"The notion still astounds me, but it feels surprisingly comfortable."

Mike extended his hand, a gesture that bordered on

downright affectionate in the De Costa family. "Then good luck to you."

Greg shook his brother's hand and punched him in the shoulder for good measure. "You're just happy my lord of the jungle act is going to take the focus off of you on bended knee for the second time in your life. Here's hoping you get it right this time."

Two punches later, Mike was out the door and zig-zagging his way through the party toward the mobile catering truck.

Leaving Greg to swig a final gulp of champagne and hope like hell he had chosen the right approach to win Jackie—for good.

Sure, it might present a bit of a challenge to venture out on a makeshift stage in front of an important client, most of his staff and the network executives in town for the weekend while he was dressed as Tarzan, lord of the jungle.

But bottom line, he would do whatever it took to win the woman he loved.

Starting right now.

JACKIE LISTENED semi-patiently to Shamus regale his small audience with stories about the production of his Back To Nature commercial. She even managed to wave her hand at the throng of people surrounding her when Shamus asked her to identify herself for the attendees.

But as the music started for the Back To Nature jingle she'd penned, there was still no sign of Greg.

As she waited for the final edit of the commercial to

flash across the white screen behind the stage, she wondered how Greg could miss a party so important to his career. Had he been that eager to avoid her?

Then, instead of the commercial rolling across the screen with her voice singing the jingle in the background, a rich baritone belted out the familiar lyrics.

"So in any situation..."

A rich, sexy baritone that sounded more suited to a smoky barroom than a cocktail party, let alone a concert hall.

"Just follow your natural inclination..."

Anticipation sang through her veins in time to the music, but nothing could have prepared her for Greg's ultimate entrance.

"And get Back To Nature with me."

Tarzan appeared on stage. Only, quite frankly, the lord of the jungle had never looked so good. Every woman present—from twenty years old to eighty—let out a collective sigh of appreciation.

Greg wore the male version of the buff-colored suede outfit Jackie had worn to film the commercial. Against his tanned skin the buttery-soft leather looked sort of Native American.

And sexy as hell.

He wore a strand of shark's teeth on a rawhide necklace, not that he needed anything to draw attention to the defined muscles of his chest.

Jackie ogled him so hard she feared for her eyeballs' position in her head. She was so consumed by the sensual appeal of Greg's surprise act, that it took her until halfway through the second stanza to realize he was putting himself on the line, in the spotlight, and very much in an unconventional position—for her.

"Just follow your natural inclination..." He slowed the tempo down as his jingle wound to a close, stopping a few inches from where she stood at the front of the low stage.

Like Elvis in Hawaii—the original king of rock at the top of his game—Greg hit his knees along with the last note, delivering them eye to eye for her.

"And get Back To Nature with me."

And Jackie was as star-struck as every woman who had ever watched Elvis sing "Aloha."

Greg wanted her. So much that he was willing to make a spectacle of himself in front of the biggest players in his corporate environment to win her.

Hope bloomed through her like a spring blossom, fragile but full of potential. A happy tear itched the back of her eye.

Like the unrestrained fan she'd always been, Jackie leaped for the man of her dreams. Throwing her arms around his neck, she kissed him until she saw stars, answering the obvious question of his song in a way no man could misinterpret.

When she finally pulled away, Greg smiled. Not disappointed in the least by the public display of affection. He drew her up on the stage with him, sharing the spotlight and all the clapping fans.

He lifted the microphone to his lips as he held her close with one arm.

"Jackie Brady is the talented composer behind the

Back To Nature jingle in addition to being the woman I love." The applause only grew.

He squeezed her hip and nudged her forward, giving her no choice but to take a small bow. Right away, the internalized voice of her mother said she should have curtsied, yet when Jackie sought her parents' faces in the crowd, she saw they were laughing and clapping too.

Her father shouted a "Brava!" that could probably be heard for miles, while her mother tossed a rose from the band of her straw hat.

Warmth, pride and so much love threatened to make her bawl her eyes out. Jackie stepped backward, finding Greg's arm just when she needed it most.

"I love you," he whispered in her ear as he guided her down the two steps on one side of the stage.

She believed him. The rightness of his words filled her. She would have been willing to walk away for him no matter how much it hurt. She would have stifled her impulsiveness for once to do what was right. But it felt so darn good that she didn't have to.

Greg wanted her just the way she was.

The real commercial music blared in the background as they sought privacy on the outskirts of the crowd. They ducked behind the palm tree ice sculpture to half hide behind the caterer's truck. No doubt the audience was being treated to the final product at this point.

Jackie didn't care. Didn't need to see it right now.

She turned to him, leaning against one side of the truck for support.

"I love you, too," she confided, launching herself

into his arms as thoroughly as he'd propelled his way into her heart. "I don't know why I didn't realize it before."

"Maybe you just needed to see it for yourself."

She trailed her fingers down his bare chest to his half naked thigh. "You sure gave me an eyeful today."

"I do what it takes to win good ratings." He stopped the adventurous journey of her fingertips with one hand. "But you're going to give the rest of the party an eyeful they definitely don't want if you keep touching me."

Slow heat simmered through her at the implication, but she couldn't help peering over one shoulder to be sure they were out of view of the rest of the partygoers.

"Then you'd better make a date to be alone with me as soon as this party is over so I have something to look forward to. But in the meantime, do you think you're going to take any heat from the network for singing to me just now?"

He leaned close to kiss her, tasting her mouth with a slow thoroughness that left her breathless for more.

"Do I look like I care?"

She tugged on one of the shark's teeth around his neck. "Frankly, no. But I wouldn't want you to lose your job because of me."

After all, she'd never meant to keep him from doing what he enjoyed most.

"Actually, those are the network execs over there," he pointed to a table of three women and a man in a perfectly creased ivory linen suit with an orchid in his lapel. "They have a sort of West Coast approach to things, so I'm thinking they're not really going to care about the Tarzan display. But for the long-term, I'm thinking about moving back to production anyway."

"Which you've loved all along." Jackie couldn't help but smile. Maybe he was thinking about making the swap for her, but she knew how much he enjoyed production and all the creativity that went behind it. Funny how it seemed they were both going to be happier in their jobs for having known one another.

"But I'm only going to be brave enough to move over to production if you get brave enough to start sending out your kids' music to a few recording companies."

"You drive a hard bargain, Tarzan." Thanks to Greg giving her more self-assurance, she just might be ready to take that risk.

"I didn't get to be lord of the jungle by going easy on people, lady. Besides, I prefer to think of it as compromising. Negotiating, even."

A surge of new confidence pulsed through Jackie as the crowd watching their commercial on the big screen broke out into applause all over again.

"Looks like our joint creative effort is a hit." Greg slid his fingers around her waist, rubbing the thin polka dot material with his palms.

Desire slid through her, all the more delicious because she knew she'd get to indulge that sultry feeling again and again. And again.

She trailed her hands across his chest, absorbing the masculine heat of him.

"Here's hoping it's the first of many, many more."

She leaned in to kiss his bottom lip, press her body to his.

The answering stirring of his body couldn't have been more obvious.

Of course, Greg's low growl warned her she was playing with fire.

"You're in big trouble for this later, woman."

She eyed the cabana and wondered if they could make it into hiding without being observed.

"Better get used to it." She tugged him toward the cabana, keeping his body close behind hers. "Didn't I tell you I'm devoted to causing a commotion?"

In the background, Jackie could hear Shamus accepting the crowd's praise and making excuses for Jackie and Greg.

She'd thank him later. Right now, she could only think about following her natural inclinations and finding a private place with Greg.

This time, she'd share more with him then ever before—heart, body and soul.

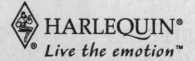

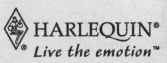

We've been making you laugh for years!

 HARLEQUIN®

Duets™

**Join the fun in May 2003
and celebrate Duets #100!
This smile-inducing series,
featuring gifted writers and
stories ranging from amusing to zany,
is a hundred volumes old.**

This special anniversary volume offers two terrific
tales by a duo of Duets' acclaimed authors.
You won't want to miss...

Jennifer Drew's You'll Be Mine in 99

and

The 100-Year Itch by Holly Jacobs

With two volumes offering two special stories every
month, Duets always delivers a sharp slice of the lighter
side of life and *especially* romance. Look for us today!

Happy Birthday, Duets!

Visit us at www.eHarlequin.com

HD100TH

If you enjoyed what you just read,
then we've got an offer you can't resist!

Take 2 bestselling love stories FREE!

Plus get a FREE surprise gift!

HARLEQUIN®

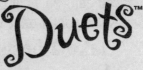 Duets™

TWO ROMANTIC COMEDIES IN ONE FUN VOLUME!

Don't miss double the laughs in

Once Smitten
and
Twice Shy

From acclaimed Duets author
Darlene Gardner

Once Smitten—that's Zoe O'Neill and Jack Carter, all right! It's a case of "the one who got away" and Zoe's out to make amends!

In *Twice Shy,* Zoe's two best friends, Amy Donatelli and Matt Burke, are alone together for the first time and each realizes they're "the one who never left!"

Any way you slice it, these two tales serve up a big dish of romance, with lots of humor on the side!

Volume #101
Coming in June 2003

Available at your favorite retail outlet.

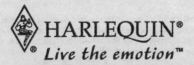

A "Mother of the Year" contest brings
overwhelming response as thousands of women
vie for the luxurious grand prize....

Kate Hoffmann

Jacqueline Diamond

Jill Shalvis

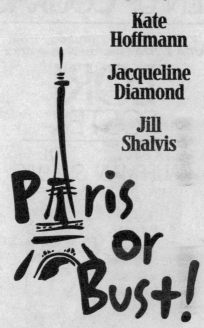

Paris or Bust!

A hilarious and romantic trio of new stories!

With a trip to Paris at stake, these women are
determined to win! But the laughs are many as three of
them discover that being finalists isn't the most
excitement they'll ever have.... Falling in love is!

Available in April 2003.

HARLEQUIN®
Makes any time special ®

Visit us at www.eHarlequin.com

PHPOB

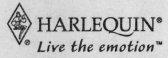